T0131491

THE HISTORY OF NEW HAMPSHIRE AND OTHER FABLES

DUNCAN CULLMAN

authorHOUSE

WHAT REALLY
MATTERS TO ME

Introduction: When the Saints Come Marching In

In the very latter days of most our lives,

When the saints come marching in, I want to be in that number when,

When I will have realized everyone who tried to help me was a saint.

I cannot even count the total number of them; they were like sand in the turbulent sea.

In my youth, of course I did not realize that adversity was sent from heaven to build me a strong character.

When I get to heaven and hang stars for God, I will need be tough.

No wimps allowed and no cowards; you will need be brave to be an angel.

Brave like those who contest the law with the rich and haughty.

They will never amount to much with God, those who put their faith in the stock market.

Be a saint and help those less fortunate than you more.

MY BROTHER GRAHAM

FINALLY I WILL GET TO SEE MY BROTHER. I SAW HIM ALMOST EVERY DAY between 1953 and 1961, except for vacations of course. Our parents were not even the same, yet we grew up in the same house. We lived under one roof, and his mother fed us all—my own father plus her husband, Graham's father. Though sometimes we ate in separate dining quarters, we usually got together after meals or to practice baseball at 6:00 a.m. before school, though that crack of the bat and yelling in the backyard upset his sleeping mother, or the sleeping neighbors, or my sleeping father.

Didn't we get enough sports at school? his mother and father wondered. My own father had other things on his mind, namely business and the stock market, plus where was he going tonight—to which cocktail party to social climb? He spoke softly to me at the breakfast table and explained the world to me from behind his newspaper he was reading, the *New York Times*.

"I was born into this world to be like my own father, who is an aristocrat. It's not our fault that we are rich and other people are poor. We are who we are to become like our own parents, not like other people who are different from us. They are the way they are for several generations. If their parents are bums, then they are bums. If a man is a house servant, than his child is more likely to be a house servant too. Your father is rich, so you will probably be too if you learn your lessons in school. You like the outdoors more, so maybe you will be an engineer."

"An FBI!" I protested. I liked to dig with my shovel in the backyard.

My mountain of dirt was an imaginary ski hill for our favorite toys, stuffed mice from Germany. They were originally manufactured to be bookmarks in Germany, but in our backyard each one had a name and an individual personality. They even won ski races like the Olympics for Mice!

Graham's original mouse was so worn from love that it lost all its hair covering. It was still shaped like a field mouse but was all the more just brown mouse leather. I always managed to lose my mice. Sometimes they went to school with me.

"What is that thing in your pocket?" screamed the elderly teacher.

"Oh, it's just my field mouse."

"Abhorrent! Put that thing away, and don't bring that back to school. Understand?"

My father would ask me to show my pet mouse to elderly ladies at our own Jewish family gatherings. I would place the mouse between my thumb and index finger and wiggle it from another finger below. The women would all scream.

Graham knew my technique, however his father, who had been in the RAF, was very strict and wouldn't let him indulge in such nonsense. I had met all his family relatives. They were all English and drank tea from the best tea cups from England or China, Singapore or Mandalay. The men had all been soldiers in the Second World War. They didn't talk about it with the women, to avoid scaring them. Sometimes at the beach, they told some war stories among themselves, and we boys could sometimes listen—unless it was grown-up talk that pertained more to business and grievances.

I spent much more time with Graham's family than with my own. Midweek I ate my meals with them in the kitchen. They were our servants, but I never looked down on them. Caroline was like my mother now that I had lost my own to the sanatorium in Great Barrington, Massachusetts. I went there with my father to visit her, but I was not allowed inside. The car was very cold, but my father probably asked if I could ski on the snow, and someone must have said they would babysit me from inside the doorway. It was snowing. I imagined my own mother was watching me, and I always remembered it that way, although she most likely was not. Finally my father came out of the building, and I did not even see my mother once.

Caroline, my governess, had nothing better to do than to love me as well. She had lost one child in childbirth, she later confessed to me, and I filled the empty space she had; I became her second child. That was very lucky for me because I was actually adopted of Anglo-Saxon origin, so I was most fortunate to be raised proper English with an English accent because the Groves were immigrants from near London, though of course Graham had been born stateside.

Frank, or actually Francis, was Graham Grove's father's name. He had loaded the ordinances on the British Spitfires in the Battle of Britain, which the Germans called Der Blitz. The English were very proud to have beaten the Germans in the war even though it had almost destroyed their empire. They had lost many colonies and lost many ships on the high seas, which were now replaced by American ships. Though they had won the war, somehow they had managed to lose the war. They all knew it, and it was a sore subject. Though the Groves had been lucky to emigrate over here where wages were higher, they had to take menial jobs like roofing, lawn cutting, and carpentry. They struggled to make ends meet. They drove English cars, like the miniature Ford, to save on gas, but the cars broke down and were not entirely reliable.

Frank had been a semipro soccer player in England and had broken his leg quite badly preventing, him from making the Professional League. It was a bitter disappointment for him but, that made him a baker in Caroline's parents pastry shop. I am sure it was a very splendid place. Graham sometimes talked about it and complained that here in America, nothing was quite as good as in England. I didn't want to hear it because I had never been there and would never go. My father had business in South America, where they also drank afternoon tea fifty and a hundred or two years ago, but the custom has regretfully stopped in these modern times.

Frank wanted us to play soccer, but we didn't have it in our own schools; my private school and his public school had only football and baseball. When my father went away, all of Graham's family came to play cricket in our backyard. The hard wooden ball struck me and gave me a slight bruise. I cried because I was, for the most part, still a baby though I was already four feet tall.

We played baseball, the all-American sport invented before the Civil War, but Frank didn't have that information. Our little league bats were so small that Frank used one hand to hit us fly balls to catch until I ran into the stone wall trying to catch a really high fly. I was knocked unconscious and got a whole week off to rest and recuperate, but then we were back out there in the yard.

"Please, Frank, hit us another one!" we cried. Eventually we took turns ourselves, with Graham hitting some to me and vice versa. Then Frank took the coaching job with the Masonic Little League Team of Royaton. I had played the previous year with the Kiwanis Team and then missed a season because I went to South America to sightsee and ski with my father and Mrs. Wing. We had gone to Machu Picchu and Cuzco in Peru and then headed to Portillo in Chile and Temuco to ski the Volcano Llaima.

The next year, my father was terribly busy and consumed a lot of bourbon whiskey, so Graham and I were the stars of Frank's winning team, and Graham was awarded the batting title. I had a fit because I calculated I had beaten him for the title by one point. I think we shared the crown eventually; it was just politics as usual that I had been overlooked.

"I don't want you to play baseball," my father, Louis, said. There was dead silence. "I have more important things for you to do," he added, but he never explained. He never explained that he was jealous that his own son was turning out to resemble more the man in the kitchen than him. Finally he thought that maybe I could learn to be a baker or a cook, and the servants might be able to train me. That never quite happened because now I dreamed only of doing sports. I found my father's old tennis racquet and hit a tennis ball against the overhead garage door until finally my father noticed it needed paint; then he forbade me to play tennis there.

I was to be shipped away to boarding school in New Hampshire. The Groves were going to England again, and their services wouldn't be needed anymore. My father had found a new fiancée, but she didn't take kindly to me even though she had two older boys of her own. The car was packed, and Frank would be driving me away to my new home at Holderness School in the White Mountains of New Hampshire. Other than one half-hour conversation nine years later, this would be the last time I would see Caroline and Frank. I waved goodbye to Graham. I was thirteen years old now and doing what my father had done when he was a young boy. His mother had shipped him off to Fessenton, Choate, and Hotchkiss. Then he had gone to Yale, an Ivy League college.

Frank was very polite and began to talk to me on the long, six-hour drive from Connecticut up into the wilds of New England. It was Labor Day, and a few leaves were already turning yellow in the picturesque, quaint New England villages. I liked seeing each and every one because I had been here many times with my own father Louis on ski trips or to visit my maternal grandparents south of Boston. Frank was almost apologetic because he sensed this would be very hard for me to suddenly move away at such a young age. In his mind, I was not mature enough to weather such a change. He was trying to console me that it would not be so bad because I would ski in winter, and yes, they would have baseball and football teams. I would be a star because he had coached me well. When I finally got out of the car and my belongings were all in my room, he gave me a hug goodbye, which he had never done before. He began to cry, and I did too. I was terrified. I missed my field mice. I missed Caroline. I missed Graham. They were my family. I would not see them anymore. I felt abandoned and deserted. Frank drove away. I followed the car with my eyes until I could no longer see it.

I was traumatized by my new surroundings. My roommate was from Pakistan and was a devout Muslim. He rolled out a carpet in our room between the beds and prayed when the sun went down, and he prayed again when the sun came up although he could not see it because our room faced north. "What are you doing?" I would inquire.

The quarterback of my football team would become a general in the Vietnam conflict and disobey orders to attack Laos, refusing to launch a full scale invasion. I would teach my Muslim roommate to box, and he would become a navy pilot on an aircraft carrier and shoot down a lot of MIGs, plus drop napalm, which bothered him to his dying day because he was a devoted Muslim and knew violence begets more violence.

I went out for passes as an end and caught them. Our baseball team was a disaster not worth mentioning, except I was the shortstop and the only one who had been trained in the sport. Of course I made the ski team too, and I was happy as a clam to see so much snow and coach my young teammates, but I had a few problems with authority. There was no psychiatrist at the school, only a nurse who kept me from dying of dehydration when I had gone with the school and made fifteen runs at Tuckerman's Ravine in one day. It almost killed me because I had forgotten to drink water. Within a year, that same nurse went through a red light in the town in thick fog and was killed by the snowplow.

I have nothing nice to say about the headmaster of that school when I attended. His name was Hagerman, and he had a beef to chew with all skiers. "There is so much more to life than skiing. You will need a job to get married and raise a family. Then there's college to think about, and the military." I would hear none of it. Ski, ski, ski. Ski free or die! That was the state motto—well, not really.

MOUSE BASEBALL, FIELD MICE WERE OUR HEROES

MY BROTHER WASN'T ACTUALLY MY BROTHER, BUT WE GREW UP IN the same house together, so we were like brothers. We had mice who were living creatures in our minds, though actually all our mice were stuffed for bookmarks and exported by West Germany.

Graham was like a brother more than most, and his mouse lineup for the big daily game was like this:

Gramps, center field, batting average .478
Pence, second base, .274
Mombourquette, catcher, .304
Whitey, first base, .461
Pluto the Dog (not a mouse), third base, .197
Geraldine, pitcher, .256
Rudy, right field, .399
Cat (not a mouse), left field, .411
Toad (not a mouse), shortstop, .246
Dewey, pinch hitter, .247

I can't seem to remember my mice nowadays because my wicked stepmother threw away all my toys the day I went to prep school. They were all in an antique trunk. She wanted the trunk for her children. I had several of these furry creatures, and for my baseball team, there were a few extra players as well that were not the treasured stuffed mice with very long tails. I had a full roster and calculated all their batting averages at least three times weekly all summer.

Their miniature bats were from pens shaped like bats sold at Yankee Stadium. The ball was a marble thrown with the left hand to the batting mouse held in the right hand, which swung the bat. Smash—the marble landed somewhere, designating what kind of hit it was. Gramps was leading in home runs a few years in a row. He was a stuffed mouse so well loved by Graham, who sucked his thumb at night still while clutching that cherished mouse.

Mouse baseball was played on the floor of the TV room at the south end of the big house, upstairs on the second floor. Usually the TV was on, and it was the New York Yankees winning again. They rarely lost in the mid-1950s.

I suppose we did manage to do our homework as well back then, and I remember "Mouse Baseball" games lasting almost to nine o'clock, our bedtime.

I would wake up at five thirty on some mornings and try to cram in my homework before school.

"What in hell do you do all night?" asked my teacher when for some reason my homework was not quite completed. I would have a favorite stuffed mouse in my pocket for luck even though I had been told never to bring them to school again.

Graham went to public grade school in Rowayton, and I think that because he was younger, he didn't have as much homework. My private school specialized in children who had been adopted. I bused forty minutes every morning to the North Stamford and New Canaan line, where the school sports fields were actually in Stamford but the school was New Canaan Country School. I heard its buildings became outdated by 1995, and they tore them all down, though I'm not sure about this.

Graham, who is now reborn and goes by Walter Groves, still has all his mice somewhere at his summer home in Alliance, North Carolina. He got involved in town politics, was elected selectman, and fought for decency—only to get sued by everybody and their uncle. Then he moved back to his main house in Atlanta, where he has a new dog, Sherlock Holmes, who is on a special diet for a stomach disorder common in that breed, English springer spaniel. Graham's wife fell off the bus, meaning she fell off the wagon too and hit the bottle, so they divorced. At least he has the dog, whom I renamed Comstock, because his eyes bulge out of his head in happiness as he consumes a giant slab of porterhouse steak and prime rib rare due to a miracle.

It's a miracle too that we two almost brothers still get to see each other seventy years later. He is now my only friend from childhood, and I am his only friend left from his childhood. We get together at the beach now because Graham has given up skiing due to his knee injury.

The waves break upon the shoreline.

"I remember, my brother, that great team we were on called Masons, or Masonics. Your dad was the coach, and we won the championship in 1960. I remember hitting only one home run or maybe two, but I was so busy running the bases that I didn't even see where the ball landed. Everyone told me it was a homerun, but I rarely hit them because I was a scrawny kid not much larger than any of those field mice who were our heroes."

The ships go by on the ocean, first a small one and then a bigger one. We went different directions most of our lives, mostly not seeing each other.

I was freezing to death in my ramshackle yurt in Twin Mountain, New Hampshire, where the temperature went down to minus forty Fahrenheit. My dog, Heidikins, was crying as the fire went out. I had a broken collarbone, and she realized we were both going to die there and then in February 1970.

Out of the deep frozen fog of that Siberia temperature came my almost brother, Graham, driving a Volkswagen bus. He was calling my name, though I hadn't seen him in ten years. My life was spared once again.

COMSTOCK GUNSTOCK

MY BROTHER, THE KID WHO GREW UP IN THE SAME HOUSE AS ME IN Darien, Connecticut, arrived at North Myrtle Beach to stay with me and my fiancée, and he brought his dog, Sherlock Holmes, an English Springer Spaniel.

"He isn't allowed to eat anything but dog food," announced my brother, laying down the rules. I hadn't seen my brother Graham in ten years since he had visited me in New Hampshire after his open-heart surgery because his doctor advised him to remain active. Stay active he did, skiing up and down the White Mountain Beer League Giant Slalom race courses, finishing next to last but still qualifying for hugely discounted lift tickets plus ski race party après-ski food, which saved us having to buy food at markets or restaurants. He didn't have Sherlock Holmes with him back then, but after a knee injury, he no longer skied. Neither did he have the wife he had brought with him on his first visit to see me in New Hampshire. She had "fallen off the bus," and he inferred she loved vodka too much.

He brought his laptop from Atlanta. I had never seen one except in the movies, where government secret agents had them. It was all very inspiring. He introduced me to Facebook, where he was "Walter Godsmark." That was his maternal grandfather's name back in England. I thought back then he must have been quite impressed by the fellow to rename himself.

It was obvious to me that he had really been born again. He was now on the cusp of being a new creature, a converted son of God, an angel in the making with a new stent in his heart. He and I were now in our seventies, which isn't a bad time to consider becoming an angel rather than going to the other place.

I looked at his dog and said, "When Sherlock turns eight years old you, may want to feed him Alpo or wet dog food that doesn't have nitrates in it." I was trying to give him some foresight into pet health for aging dogs.

"Sherlock Holmes just eats dog food," he repeated, and he then ordered the dog to lie down. This was what had happened to him as a child, basically. His own father had been very strict and told him to finish his dinner plate of meat and potatoes, eating every last morsel because people were starving in China.

Graham grew up a little pudgier than me, but now we were both a bit too heavy.

"I have been on the dog diet." I told him about saving food on my every plate for my dog to eat. "My last dog, JP, lived to be fifteen years old on human food."

"My dog doesn't need human food because my vet says he has digestive problems and should eat special dog food!"

We went to the beach with the dog, who sat on my lap in the front passenger seat with his head out the window. Then we parked and headed for the breaking waves, with the dog barking loudly as he ran into the salt water, drinking it a bit as dogs do. I threw the tennis ball in my bag, and the dog chased it.

"Oh, he is a bird dog. Fetch!" Susan, my wife, threw the ball, and Sherlock chased it. Then we all returned to our beach chairs to sit with Graham, now Walter, sitting in his beach chair. The dog threw up immediately.

"He has stomach problems! Sit, Sherlock!" he commanded. The dog sat down but saw the distant tennis ball and barked.

Eventually we had our fill of sand and sun and headed to the King of Crabs Restaurant—all you can eat. I snuck an empty plastic shopping bag into my pocket before leaving his van. Susan smiled at me. We loved Sherlock as well as Walter and we are all one big family reunited now despite this pandemic of 2020.

We waited six feet apart, and servers filled our plates from the buffet for us. I polished off king crab and oysters, as did Walter. Susan ate chicken and prime rib. The prime rib looked really juicy, so I headed for seconds.

There were ice cream cones, and Walter had a cheesecake. There was no way I was going to eat this huge piece of juicy prime rib, so I loaded it into my handy plastic shopping bag and put it in my pocket. Susan saw me, smiling. The waiter returned, and we paid the check and left. Sherlock was waiting in the van with windows rolled down. Luckily it was a cloudy, but this was May, not the dead of summer.

"My brother, this has been real. It's very good to see you again, and I hope you go to Manpower and recruit a female carpenter's helper who stays on the bus, so to speak!" I said to distract him slightly while Susan was reaching in the plastic bag I had passed her and digging out the huge slab of prime rib.

The dog's tail began wagging, but Walter was busy watching traffic. I didn't know when we would be seeing both Walter and Sherlock again.

"Comstock Gunstock," I call the happy little dog who was turning seven. I decided to rename him now. It was as if though he had been born again now that the prime rib reached his belly. He had new life, and like Walter, he was waiting for God to call him home, as we all are.

MAN WITH CAMEL, 9

ONCE AGAIN, OUR MAN IS CROSSING THE DESERT. IT'S A VERY GOOD thing that he has this camel for a friend, because the desert is very hot and very arid.

Over the sand dunes they come, and lo and behold, ahead of them they see an airport. Big, fancy jets are landing and taking off. There is a control tower whose air-traffic controllers spot the man and his camel and then radio airport security to check them out. Our man might be a terrorist, and the camel may be a robot bomb. Who knows? So here they come with Berettas in Land Cruisers and Toyotas to question our man and his camel.

The camel lets out a huge screech and farts a tremendous cloud of cactus gas.

Our man removes his hat and puts his hands up in the air. "Don't shoot! It's just me and my camel!"

"Identify yourself and where have you come from. Who sent you here?" they demand.

"I have come from Allah as a messenger to tell you the very good news!" says our man.

"Now, what would that be? Are you a madman from the desert? If you are a Bedouin, where is your flock?"

"I have been sent by Allah to inform you that the day of reckoning and judgment has arrived, and men who carry automatic rifles will use them on themselves out of guilt because the Prophet has appeared before their very eyes, and they should welcome him with a huge banquet and give great thanks to Allah for sending a contrite and humble servant of the Lord into their vary midst, whereby they might rejoice in saving his life from the wildebeest and the desert, from which he has come bringing salvation and the very words that Allah has spoken into his ears when he almost died of starvation and dehydration. Make a straight pathway in the desert, for the Lord is coming—a humble man from among the followers of God who likewise lives on locusts and honey. The time is at hand for repentance and conversion to the faith. God alone can save you, not your bullets!"

After deciding that the man was a kook of some kind who had spent too many days in the hot sun, they invited him to the infirmary to bandage his cuts and abrasions and to water his camel.

If ever you come among total strangers, you are to do the same. Make an announcement that it must be divine guidance that has delivered you to meet new friends everywhere you go, and most likely they will feed you and house you, at least overnight, whereby you can recuperate from the hot sun. Your entire life shall indeed be like a man crossing a great desert. Some people will help you on your journey if you let them. They are very curious about where you have come from and what you have seen. Their lives are like long journeys through wastelands as well. The Earth is not such a hospitable place, and should you find a companion like a dog or a cat, or even a camel, feel privileged and treat your friends well. It will be written upon your face that you are a happy man because you know God, who is most righteous. You want to be holy like God, love everyone everywhere, and spread the good news of salvation that God cares about us like a father cares for his children, like a mother cares for her newborn. Go in peace, because God sends you forward.

MY ST. FRIEND (HAVE CONFIDENCE IN GOD)

My friend, who is more precious than wine, if I have lost you, then let me drink wine and remember just how precious our time together is.

Trust that the God you pray to has ears.

Have confidence in your God, whose knowledge far surpasses your own,

That He will deliver you from evil if you ask to be delivered.

He will make you victorious in this your new day,

For underfoot of the righteous is the Holy Land.

Where you are now standing is where He has intended you to be.

If there is danger, He will instruct you to run away.

It is not a safe place, the Earth, and that is why you are given feet,

That you might flee the tornado and outrun the flood.

Your people are those who surround you daily, your friends.

If they stand in the distance, they have lost confidence in you.

Why should they doubt that God protects us all?

His very angels are at work, directing the daily traffic

To make you safe on your travels here in this dangerous world.

He will not deliver you to the enemy while you still have a mission

To glorify His name among the people in many faraway places.

The tree cannot flee from the lumberjack. Take heed—you are no tree.

You have learned to read the newspaper; you see new clouds on the horizon.

The wind is shifting, so set your sails to accommodate our new tempest.

Where you are standing, you are meant to stand, and where you travel,

You are meant to travel to make new friends.

Because perhaps your old friends are jealous of the success God has granted you,

You cannot bring them all with you, only those who love you.

They hear God; when you speak, you mention God.

You mention that God shall direct us to save ourselves

Because God is with us now; we are His people

Due to the remission of sin by the sacrifice of the Lamb who has died

For us in our place, that we may feast and live at least until tomorrow.

That is entirely a different day when we may be asked to sacrifice our own greed once again

In order to serve others, in order to follow like sheep or maybe to lead like the pastor.

I am sorry and apologize to every friend I left behind; I did not serve you better.

I was egocentric, serving myself, and perhaps was not a good listener to all your pleas for help.

So now we are each alone and no longer together as a team.

Please come back to me, if you hear my voice, then be reassured.

I have not forgotten you; I think of you and remember the good times,

Our conversations to break the silence because God did not want us to be alone forever.

He has gathered us here to be together in this His synagogue, His temple, His chapel, His cathedral, or His mosque—

Or should we invent our own religion?

Or beneath this great pine tree to shade us, or an oak,

Here in the house of the Lord where you live, because if God cannot live here also in your home, neither shall you.

Have confidence in God that He resides here with you, if you obey His commandments.

Worship no other God before Me, says your God.

You left your former friends because they heard a distant drummer somewhere.

Not everyone can sing your song, but keep singing anyway,

Because God hears you and delights your joy; your God reinforces you even if you are a hermit.

Elijah fled the city and all the people to sit under a small shade tree in the desert,

Where God spoke to him and said,

"Get up and go, Elijah. Go prophesize the very good news that salvation is near for those who repent."

Yes, let us repent our wicked ways and come together as one people united, not divided.

Let us rejoin the circle of God's love given to us through us to rejoin hearts and hands.

We can rebuild these lasting friendships to serve one another and the common good,

Not just our own selfish needs. Because you, my friend, are the best investment I ever made.

God is my friend as well because He directed me in your direction.

He has given me that I may lay down my own life for you.

You are thankful and gracious to have a friend like me sent from God.

I am thankful and gracious to be able to wash your feet lovingly.

Thank you for being my friend, even though we barely met and talked but a few days.

Our destinies on Earth pulled us apart into different directions; even so,

May God gladly reunite us one day. Let us be hopeful …

HAVE CONFIDENCE IN GOD (HABEN SIE VERTRAUEN IN GOTT)

Vertrauen, dass Gott sie zu beten hat Ohren

Haben Sie Vertrauen in Ihrem Gott, dessen Wissen weit übertrifft Ihre eigenen

Das Er wird dich von dem Bösen, wenn Sie geliefert werden, bitten

Er wird Sie in diesem in den neuen Tag als Sieger

Für unter den Füßen des Gerechten ist das Heilige Land

Wo du stehst jetzt, wo er euch sein soll

Wenn es gefährlich ist, wird er Sie anweisen, wegzulaufen

Es ist kein sicherer Ort der Erde, und das ist, warum Sie gegeben Füße

Dass Sie den Tornado und hinter sich lassen, die Flut könnte fliehen

Ihre Leute sind diejenigen, die Sie täglich umgeben, Ihre Freunde

Wenn sie in der Ferne stehen haben sie verlorenes Vertrauen in Sie

Warum sollten sie daran zweifeln, daß Gott schützt uns alle?

Seine sehr Engel sind bei der Arbeit des täglichen Verkehr regeln

Damit Sie auf Ihren Reisen hier in dieser gefährlichen Welt sicher

Er wird dich nicht an den Feind liefern, während Sie noch eine Mission haben

Seinen Namen unter den Menschen in vielen weit entfernten Orten zu verherrlichen

Der Baum kann nicht von dem Lumberjack fliehen, beherzigen Sie sind kein Baum

Sie gelernt haben, die Zeitung zu lesen, sehen Sie neue Wolken am Horizont

Der Wind Verschiebung so eingestellt Ihre Segel unseren neuen Sturm accommodate

Wo Sie Sie stehen sollen stehen und wo Sie reisen

Sie sind zu reisen bedeutet, neue Freunde zu finden

Weil vielleicht deine alten Freunde neidisch auf den Erfolg sind Gott hat dir einige

Man kann sie nicht mit dem du alle, nur die, die lieben Sie

Sie hören Gott, wenn Sie sprechen Sie Gott erwähnen

Sie erwähnen, dass Gott wird uns direkt um sie zu retten, weil

Weil Gott mit uns ist, jetzt sind wir sein Volk

Durch die Vergebung der Sünde durch das Opfer des Lammes, der gestorben ist

Für uns in unserem Ort, dass wir zumindest bis morgen Fest und leben

Das ist ganz ein anderer Tag, wenn wir unsere eigene Gier gebeten werden, wieder zu opfern

Um andere zu dienen, um wie Schafe zu folgen oder vielleicht wie der Pfarrer führen

Es tut mir leid und ich entschuldige mich hinter jedem Freund verlassen, ich habe dienen Sie nicht besser

Ich war egozentrisch mich dienen und vielleicht nicht ein guter Zuhörer zu Ihrem Hilferuf

So, jetzt sind wir jeweils allein und nicht mehr als Team zusammen

Bitte komm zurück zu mir, wenn du meine Stimme hören, dann beruhigt sein

Ich habe sie nicht vergessen, ich denke an dich und an die guten Zeiten erinnern

Unsere Gespräche das Schweigen zu brechen, weil Gott uns nicht wollte, für immer allein sein

Er hat uns hier versammelt in diesem Sein synagogue zusammen zu sein Sein Tempel Seine Kapelle Seine Kathedrale

Oder unter diesem großen Kiefer zu schattieren uns oder einer Eiche

Hier im Hause des Herren, wo Sie leben, denn wenn Gott nicht hier lebt auch in Ihrem Hause, Dich Soll

Haben Sie Vertrauen in Gott, dass er hier bei dir wohnt, wenn Sie seine Gebote befolgen

Keinen andern Gott anbeten vor mir sagt, dein Gott,

Sie haben Ihre früheren Freunde, weil sie einen fernen Schlagzeuger irgendwo gehört

Nicht jeder kann dein Lied singen, aber immer singen trotzdem

Weil Gott Sie hört und erfreut Ihre Freude, euer Gott, stärkt Sie, auch wenn Sie ein Einsiedler sind

Elia floh die Stadt und die ganze Volk unter einem kleinen Baum Schatten in der Wüste zu sitzen

Wo Gott zu ihm sprach, sagte,

„Steh auf und geh, Elia das eine sehr gute Nachricht go prophezeien, dass das Heil für die in der Nähe ist, die nicht umkehrt

Ja lasst uns unsere bösen Wegen umkehren und kommen zusammen als ein Volk nicht vereinigt geteilt

Lassen Sie uns den Kreis der Liebe Gottes zu uns durch uns wieder zusammenzubringen Herzen und Hände gegeben schließen

Wir können diese dauerhaften Freundschaften wieder aufzubauen sie und das Gemeinwohl dienen

Nicht nur unsere eigenen egoistischen Bedürfnisse, weil du mein Freund die beste Investition, die ich je gemacht

Gott ist mein Freund als auch, weil er führte mich in Ihre Richtung

A MAN AND A
CAMEL, PART 10

AMAN IS CROSSING THE DESERT ON HIS CAMEL. HE HAS DONE THIS A dozen times at least. It is another bright, sunshiny, bluebird day, but no birds live here. They would fry.

There is a dry mountain range in the far distance and what appears to be a canyon halfway to the mountains. Maybe there was water here three thousand years ago.

Velakovsky wrote that book *Worlds in Collision*. He speculated maybe the poles of planet Earth had shifted twelve degrees from around Iceland to their present location, and evidence of this shift would be that magnetic north reflects where the North Pole used to be. The land of Israel may have been more like forty degrees north latitude until the walls of Jericho came tumbling down. The Earth, it was rumored in the Bible, had experienced a slight delay in rotation and now spins slower, so people nowadays live only one hundred years old, but back before the changeover, they lived to be 160 years old in the Holy Scriptures (Old Testament)

Our man is thinking about all this as he approaches the big canyon on his camel and rides almost to its edge, though the camel is far less enthusiastic to be standing on top of a cliff with a hot desert wind.

The man is wondering just how he will cross this great expanse, which is only one of an endless number of them on each continent. He remembers that Evel Knievel was going to ride over on his motorcycle, which would be propelled by rockets to high enough altitude that he would deploy a parachute. Everyone waiting, holding his or her breath, and then some mechanical failure ensued, and Evel Knievel chickened out, more or less.

When we are going to leave this world, return to heaven to be with God, leave our material bodies behind, and have astral bodies to go home to our Lord and Creator (which some nonbelievers call death), then we will learn exactly how to make this big jump from one side of the canyon to another to be, with all our relatives who have gone before us. We will see them again. We all hope so.

So meanwhile on this Earth, we are being challenged by distances, gorges, and mountain ranges, to prepare us for our inevitable moment when we shall be once again with God on Mount Zion.

The camel is following an animal trail down through the rocks. The camel knows where to go. This is no dumb camel, whose ancestors have survived thousands upon thousands of years in this harsh environment. The man is simply along for the ride. He lets the camel show its camel genius and the way and the truth and the life, and they will live and survive.

MAN AND CAMEL 10B

WHAT IS TROUBLING ABOUT DEATH IS THERE IS NO GENETIC MEMORY of it. No one has done it and come back (although Jesus, it is rumored, has risen and will continue to return).

The camel's ancestors crossed all these gorges and mountain ranges, so there is genetic memory like that in migratory birds, perhaps.

Everyone knows what it is like to be constipated and take a great big shit. This is our clue to the big event.

We shall take a great big one, and not just poop but shit away our entire bodies when shall die, because our bodies will have served their purpose. We will shed our cocoons like moths. We will fly astrally like butterflies unto our God, whom we shall behold.

SANTA ALEXANDRIA, "WHAT REALLY MATTERS TO ME"

What really matters to me is that Alexandria Ocasio-Cortez was overlooked by the DNC.

What really matters is that the United Nations scientific study says,

"We have only twelve years to fix climate change, after which there will be no turning back."

"That global warming will irreversibly make this planet inhospitable to all mammals."

That the same middle-of-the-road politicians who have done nothing to address this issue

Are the candidates of both major parties, who are in denial of our climate crisis.

This really matters to me, and future generations, that these existentialists

Do not really care about you and me or future generations but are supported

By human greed and the corporations, with their shareholders who really don't give a damn.

These "great Americans making America great again" turn their backs exactly like the Germans did with Hitler.

Hitler was making Germany great again, building concentration camps for all dissidents protesting war and racism.

The "silent majority" has now been silenced by corporate interests who run television.

The corporations have bought our government, and the stock market was surging at the expense of our environment.

Corporate and personal profits were running out of control with the temperature.

What really matters to me is that there may be a payback to building concentration camps on our southern borders

Separating children and mothers, fathers and sons—everyone wants to come here to the USA.

The standard of life is better here than three-quarters of the world,

Which lives in famine, pestilence, and tyranny already made worse by hurricanes drought and floods from global warming elsewhere—and tornados, hurricanes, and floods here also, not to mention earthquakes from fracking.

What really matters to me is the world's refugee crisis and overpopulation, which we can no longer sustain with soaring temperatures.

That our government of the people was up for sale from day one to corporate and private interests of those with money and stuffing their pockets with more—but this is seen as normal by the news.

What can it possibly matter that we turn a blind eye to this corruption that evades justice?

This administration, whose cronies are above the law, walking free from prison due to coronavirus, to home arrest instead,

Where they read the *Wall Street Journal* like strategic investors in silk pajamas.

The children in this country are not even going to school, and that's what matters to me.

That everyone is now home alone, cut off from friends and family, being told what to do by Dr. Fauci and Drs. Trump and Pence.

This is a very dangerous world indeed, on the verge of self-destruction.

If this doesn't matter to me, I am either very rich or very senile as well and have no conscience,

No conscience at all, like 66 percent of the politicians in Washington, DC.

They have studied the law with the intention of finding loopholes around it to aggrandize themselves.

There is an overabundance of wickedness and no shame to be found in these people.

It matters to God, who will send a plague into Egypt and Babylon.

The cries of the poor and oppressed are heard in faraway heaven.

Justice will come fast and swift like an eagle, like a lion after its prey.

The children of the Lord will be vindicated and win on that great day, which will be very soon.

There will be wailing and gnashing of teeth, but I will deliver My own, says the Lord, because it matters to I Am that I Am.

On that day, journalists will be astounded that advertising won't save anything.

Will it matter to me when the wicked face what God has in store for them?

There will be a fresh dawn without them, and their names will be omitted from every history book.

The statues they erect of themselves will be torn down, as well and every street renamed.

What really matters to me is my impatience to see justice done.

There might even be forgiveness for those who mend their ways.

The liars, however, will never see the truth nor God, and this matters greatly to the rest of us,

Who will see God! Who will see God?

HISTORY OF
THE WORLD

BILLIONS OF YEARS AGO, HOT SWIRLING GASES CONTRACTED IN SPACE to form matter as we know it: that which is under gravitational control and by sheer density tremendous heat was released and ignited, forming giant stars from which light was then born.

Of course, without eyes we would not see these beams of light. This is just a history of our world relating to us humans, as we perceive it.

Furthermore, this is just my history of my own world—very subjective indeed, because I am writing all this from my sensory perception of it. It smells offensive to me only if it endangers me, and then sometimes there is no smell at all, but it is still toxic because it might be very inorganic. This is really only the history of my own little world because if you were to ask God or whoever created it, the answer might be totally unrecognizable.

Lemurs and apes, my ancestors, were evolved from amphibians who had survived partly under the water during the great cataclysm, probably from an asteroid that had rendered the land masses of the Earth unlivable.

By trial and error in a process we call Darwinism, the clever survived and the unclever perished, which suggests our very own dogs and cats are much smarter than we give them credit for.

The monkeys began to stand erect, and this had some advantages as well as disadvantages, resulting in chiropractors. Our anterior feet became dexterous hands. We learned to work with our hands, and this gave birth to weapons for fighting and eventually the industrial revolution. All this created goods and services, which became cheaper with popular demand. Translated, popular demand means a product goes down in cost per item if you produce four billion of them.

At first, everyone fought, and the strong killed the weak. This, however, was replaced by law and order, which created more consumers and thriving economies to the extent that humans dominated the Earth in great abundance.

Yet the more humans populated the planet, the more they became a host to other living organisms, bacteria and viruses among these now very numerous parasitic contagion.

Humans, by their very numerical superiority, thus became an endangered species due to various plagues and pandemics, which were created mostly by the overpopulation of humans.

If humans go extinct, then there shall be no human history of the planet save only a few books that might be discovered and decoded by whoever or whatever of intelligence might replace us, but probably not in any immediate future.

Everything of plant and animal nature upon the Earth lives and dies, unlike the diamonds that seem to be almost indestructible but are not any life form that we can relate to, unless one is born a jeweler. Therefore our history is temporal and we are existential, living here now temporarily, not permanently. We are guests of here and now but not necessarily any time far into the future. We are like the grass that grows in the morning but wilts in the hot afternoon sun.

I was born from my mother's womb, but roughly half of my genes came from my father. We are predominantly male and female or both, not asexual. In the history of my world, there is attraction between various organisms that have sex. Only the aspen or poplar trees reproduce without sex, so inform me, please, of any other asexual living organisms like those. Maybe the amoeba divides and cells divide and viruses divide. Let me know ASAP.

I am eager to learn the history of my world so I can record it for my children, who probably already know more than I do, so they each will write their own histories.

Your history is still another matter, and should we have the great pleasure to meet, I agree to be all ears, believe what you say, and then record it with my pen or keyboard.

I am not sure whether we'll make history together or write simultaneous chapters, unless of course we fall in love or travel somewhere together. In such a case, we may still have individual friends as well as common friends. Their histories may or may not become manifest should they choose to communicate their very vast experiences, which might greatly humor us and cause us to laugh uncontrollably.

There are tears to be shed as well due to our misunderstanding of one another. Sometimes we are seemingly separated by events beyond our own control, by accidents of nature, or by misunderstandings.

Please do write me often and tell me what exactly has happened, because my guesswork is rather shoddy. I confess I cannot read your mind from a distance, nor do I have eyes in the back of my head. Be more vocal and shout out at me, "I love you. I still love you and miss your many stories. I miss your rich history. I miss your own personal version of all history. I miss you, please write!"

Yours truly,
Me

ROGER AND THE
BIG JUMP

WE WERE TALKING ABOUT THE BIG JUMP FROM THIS LIFE TO THE next. We will take a really big dump and not just release feces but jump right out of our tired, old bodies and into new, immortal bodies.

Praise the Lord that we may indeed be liberated from all this disappointment on the Earth. We make so many plans, and maybe 10 percent of them come true to resemble our original dreams.

We met Roger in Santa Fe, New Mexico, and he was a very big boy from New Jersey or somewhere. He was at least twenty-four years old, so by all appearances he was a man. He ate like a man as well. "Give me two breakfast omelettes and two steak dinners!" he would tell the waitresses. He had to eat twice as much as everyone else to feed that big body of his. We were amazed any one person could eat so much. He had to weigh 290 pounds, maybe 300, and he wanted us to take him skiing in Colorado up to our cabin at just under 12,000 feet elevation.

Before we left town, however, we were sitting in a bar, and two very greasy-looking "Hermanos de La Raza Unida" were standing nearby our table and eyeing my fiancée, who was the best-looking young lady of Spanish blood their glaring eyeballs had ever beheld. Maybe they were high on something, so they pulled out their switchblades and offered to cut us up in the parking lot and leave us for the vultures. Roger's mouth dropped, but I decided to shatter my beer bottle and stand up to their bullshit. Glass went flying in all directions. They decided to leave immediately.

Off we drove with Roger toward Gladstone, Colorado, above Silverton, six hours northward across Indian Reservations through Durango and up over snowy Coal Bank Pass. Then we went down a cliff of switchbacks then and onto a well-maintained gravel road to the mine a mile and a half below my cabin. Snow was everywhere but not on the road because it was late May.

"You expect me to go up there? That's too steep!" exclaimed Roger.

My fiancée egged him on to show some manliness. "Oh, you can do it, big fella!"

"You don't have to ski down that steep mountainside. There is a road that zigzags and is perfect for doing the snowplow," I insisted.

Up the mountainside, we climbed on the little switchback road mostly with our skis on. Roger was not very happy about the long walk up to the treeline. He had been to ski areas in New Jersey and the Catskills but had never skied in the high Rocky Mountains. All three hundred pounds of his manliness would not let him chicken out now. He expected a nice, warm, cozy bed like Vail or Aspen waiting for him somewhere, perhaps in a ski movie he had seen.

We trudged upward, all three of us dumb, dumber, and dumbest, until he beheld the quaint little ten foot by ten foot cabins with homemade doors and marmot dropping interiors that had to be swept. I lit a fire for him in the military potbelly stove, which soon went out. Luckily for him, he had three hundred pounds of fat to keep him warm while shivering and burning off at least five pounds that night. He woke up invigorated, with the sun not quite risen over the mountain but at least shining on distant peaks.

"Here we go!" I exclaimed.

"We'll meet you at the bottom, Roger!" my fiancée promised as she jumped over some tree branches and went down the forty-degree slope into the Engelmann spruce forest.

"It was all her idea to bring him here!" I thought to myself as I followed her. We waited in the car for over an hour, wondering whether the coyotes had had Roger for breakfast up at the treeline somewhere.

Then he appeared out of nowhere with the skis we had loaned him broken in his arms from simultaneous ski crashes down the mountainside. Possibly he had burned off another ten pounds with all his adrenalin released.

To put it mildly, he wasn't very happy. Yet we were smiling and relieved not to be facing counts of manslaughter. My fiancée and future wife laughed hysterically. Roger was furious but decided to eat a double order of pancakes, with sausage one order and bacon on the other. He still wasn't smiling—actually, he was shaking his fist at us as we drove off, leaving him with some newfound friend to console him that we were mad people whom he should never have followed in the first place.

MAN AND CAMEL, PART 12

A MAN AND HIS CAMEL ARE CROSSING THE DESERT. HE IS THINKING about the last time he saw his older brother. They were together at Myrtle Beach on a bluebird day with the waves crashing and his brother's dog barking at the tennis ball in the sand.

That was just before the pandemic of 2020, when people still hugged and shook hands. There were contact sports and stadiums full of cheering stands. Then the SARS-CoV-2 virus came, and everyone was ordered to stay home except for essential shopping. Some cities imposed curfews, and people protested while many elderly people were dying. There was nowhere to store the bodies except in refrigerator trucks. There were mass graves. He had thought he might go sailing off on the high seas, but the desert might be easier. All he needed was a camel …

The man came into a village with an oasis. He was thirsty, and the camel drank water too. Luckily, he still had some money to pay for the water, which was expensive, when into the oasis came another rider. Lo and behold, it was his youngest brother on a camel.

"My brother, where have you come from out of the wide, dry desert?" They were both laughing and amazed to find one another here in the middle of nowhere at this water hole. His brother drank some water, and his camel drank too.

It was another glorious bluebird day in the desert. The sun was up in the sky, and it was hot. They all sought some shade at an outdoor restaurant. Someone had a recent newspaper from the outside world.

The pandemic was officially the worst ever. Three million had died in Egypt. There was no good news except the weather. A sandstorm in the forecast was thought to have quieted down. There was some Morraccan decaffeinated coffee they ordered to drink, with sandwiches of salami. Life was good when one could still get a cup of coffee!

Evening came, and they stayed in the village until dark, but the hotel was too expensive, so they rode off together under the stars. They had no news of the oldest brother, who had gone surfing in Hawaii They missed him now.

At least they were together for the moment. At least they were still alive.

THE NEW NORMAL,
ROUND ONE: DIVERSIFY

Many of us think this pandemic is the new abnormal.

We are waiting for it to be over and for our former way of life to return.

Yes, there will probably be a lull in this virus war.

People will relax and mingle and feel safe for a little while.

Then another virus will emerge, or this one will mutate.

So guess what you will need to accept in order to survive well and be happy?

This pandemic itself has created the new normal; there is no going back.

The world is overpopulated and consumes too much fossil fuel,

To the degree that our own ecosystem is endangered.

This pandemic has cured all our excessive ills.

The price of a barrel of oil has just hit an modern all-time low.

Everyone is trying to work from home.

Families are closer together than since the War of 1812.

The rest of my own life is not so many years.

I doubt very much that this nightmare we call human life will change very much.

From the World Wars to the Korean War to the Vietnamese conflict to Kuwait to Bosnia to Iraq and Afghanistan,

There has been a continuum of suffering.

It's a dismal forecast I paint, and no rosy picture.

There was the Hundred Years War and the American Civil War and the Revolutionary War, plus the War of Roses and the Napoleonic Wars.

The Black Plague and the Spanish Influenza—accept all this misery

As our unfailing human condition and live for the brief moment.

Stay safe and be healthy with good habits that promote your well-being.

Try to remain vigilant, and do not fall asleep in this constant world of danger.

What was yesterday is no more than a dream, a faint memory, and yet

The sun will rise on your new day and the moon for your new night.

Be careful, diversify, be a good soldier!

We are in the first battle of another long war.

OUTDOOR DINING MAY BE THE TEMPORARY SOLUTION FOR SAVING THE RESTAURANTS THROUGH THANKSGIVING

OUTDOOR DINING MAY BE THE ONLY REALISTIC CHANCE OF SAVING America's many restaurants. Of course, it would mean closing many main streets in many towns and cities and diverting traffic. Seating can be more spread out, but what is to prevent servers from passing the virus, unless the food can be delivered to tables in to-go boxes before customers are seated?

By Thanksgiving it will become too chilly. By then, will restaurants have enough cash flow to remain in business?

Maybe the servers should be young and healthy, wearing masks?

VISIONS OF THE GREEN PRINCE (OF LUND) ON MIDSUMMER NIGHT: GREEN LEAVES BLOOMING

Visions of the Green Prince, who sees green leaves blooming.

The long night of human madness
Must end, or man will perish.
So now must come the dawn of human awakening.

The system of greed and pollution must be compromised,
Or the planet will become something we no longer recognize as our own
Because we will not even exist.

While traveling abroad, I have been reborn in spirit
At the prospect of a world green revolution.

Because corporate greed
Is destroying our way of a healthy lifestyle.

The United States has become the sickest dog
In the pack of hounds running wildly.

People are encouraged there
Not to walk or bicycle, but to drive fast luxury cars
To Walmart, where they park in handicap parking and
Ride electric wheelchairs through the endless aisles
Because they have lost the use of their feet.

This lifestyle of heart attack stroke and cancer
Must be averted by the followers and proponents of the green revolution.

And this mindless architecture of misadventure needs to be taken back
to the drawing board and recreated by
Proponents of life, not death!

So what needs to be done is for the people to seize their governments,
Take control of their governments,
Be responsible for themselves.

This will not be an easy task.
Individually, we cannot accomplish much politically.
We will need to create a worldwide party in this endeavor.

Each of us was once lost in the darkness of material consumption.
From this, we fell ill,
Became depressed and burdened
By anxiety.

But now we see the light;
It is bright and shining
Like the sun.
We will raise high our green standards (banners).
This world is not just for corporate CEOs;
It is our world too.
We must take it back!

There is a green prince or princess in each and every one of us.
We must look inside ourselves
To find the strength to rid ourselves and the planet
Of this corporate plague.

We must have government of the people, for the people,
So help us God that we as a green nation of the living
Do not perish in a perishing world,
Because life is essential to us.
Therefore, raise high your green banner of truth and the way.
Be of clean conscience and be cleansed.
There are people like Bernie Sanders whom we endorse;
He is a prophet
Before his time.
So are we.

The proponents of big business do not like to hear
What we have to say
Because the gargantuan hospitals
Will go broke without patients.

Here at the Lund train station,
There are three thousand bicycles,
So this might be considered
The capital of something very good brewing.

The wind is shifting in our direction,
And like brave Vikings,
We shall all raise our green mast and sail.
God be with us and against those who destroy the planet!

After all, our health is more important than wealth.

FRANCONIA DOG
STORY 2B

TO SWEETEN HIS NASTY DISPOSITION. **T**HERE IS A GIANT HD television screen beaming the Bloomberg channel with business news, much of which is not good. The market has fallen; the stocks have rebounded slightly but not enough to cover their losses. My owner, Finneus, is pulling on his beard in perplexity and scratching his head (hopefully not my doggy fleas). The stock market just climbed three hundred points. Yippee, we will be going to Walmart on a spending spree, where O will get a new flea collar or a leather collar with hideous bells, like cow bells, or a big new bag of GMO-free dog food, and maybe a new dog toy. I am a senior dog now, but he still calls all us dogs his babies. I limp quite a lot from jumping into and out of the oversize Ford L350 pickup with oversized mud tires.

I used to chase fly balls in the outfield at softball every summer long, seven days a week. My master is now middle-aged as well. When I was a puppy, he was younger and more playful, so was I too. I used to run up and down the ski trails in the winter because he used to climb them at night and in the daylight. We used to do a lot more adventurous things, but I think he has developed a thyroid disorder, hypothyroidism, which has slowed him considerably. Is there a doctor in the house, or at the hospital, who can diagnose his disorder? Oh, please, great Dog in the Sky, help us all!

WILD SIDE

WILD SIDE OF FRANCONIA, BETHLEHEM, AND SUGAR HILL, NEW Hampshire's Hippy Era

Once Brian Pendleton married Esther Rosemary Wineglass, the woman of his dreams from Switzerland, in a ceremony in the apple orchard near his pillared mansion (it looked like the one in *Gone with the Wind*), Craig Millar decided the same by marrying a rock and roll star named Marguerite under the same apple tree a month later.

She was the solo vocalist in a very heavy metal band, and it was short-lasting, hot, and heavy until a few weeks later, when she ran away with the lead guitarist of her band—a very logical conclusion to marrying a rock star vocalist!

Craig, on the rebound, looked instead for a more stable woman and hooked up with the x-Ray technician from Sugar Hill Hospital, Debbie. They promptly had two children, Duncan Bean and Darcy Marie.

Craig, still reliving finer moments of the Vietnam War, where he served on Hamburger Hill in the DMZ for the Third Marine Division when they were overrun by the enemy, had nonstop drinking binges that usually involved the now separated, newly divorced Brian Pendleton, his fellow ski patrol buddy. Debbie was nursing and sleepless, the babies were crying past midnight, and so the marriage was now ending because Debbie had laid down the law and given ample unheeded warnings.

Debbie found Roger, a hardworking parcel post delivery man and nighttime Sno-Cat driver at Bretton Woods Ski Area. Then she had a third child by Roger, Hillary Princess.

Meanwhile, Craig, having partial custody of his now growing children, introduced them both to the finer things in life: beer and marijuana. Little Duncan and Darcy would return home to Roger and Debbie quite high on marijuana and drunk on beer. Next was the usual scenario of children with a stepfather sending them to their respective rooms for chores and homework left undone. Soon it was an all-out war!

Duncan Millar, as a thirteen-year-old, moved out into the woods, building primitive lean-tos, adding woodstoves and hoses, and connecting water from streams to abandoned sinks now finding new purpose. Of course, out there it was an ongoing, nonstop party: drugs, alcohol, classmates, and rebellion!

At this point, Duncan's cousin Adom decided on a lifetime career of drug dealing because he was going from heavy metal concert to heavy metal concert, with little Duncan, now almost fully grown, accompanying the entourage of young, aspiring businessmen. Darcy also joined because there was an oversupply of local hippies who had or were attending Franconia College and learning how to cultivate a cash crop like marijuana. Among other things, they learned how to cultivate marijuana to get through the never-ending local hard times of nonexistent employment.

Thus Duncan and Adom found themselves on tour with the Grateful Dead, Led Zeppelin, Jefferson Airplane, and ZZ Top. Jack was there too, writing songs for those groups, but not Sam, who preferred hunting.

Adom, with his profits soaring, bought himself a Chevy Camaro so he and his girlfriend, Rosetta Goldband, could cruise around with hay bales of pot grown by her mother deep in the Sugar Hill and Easton Valley woods now being visited by the sheriff's posses. Thus, Adom decided to improve his image of success by purchasing a Porsche 911-S; starting his own political party, The Youngerboods; and getting a pilot's license.

Finally, the police began to notice that hitherto impoverished, underemployed, crew-cut children were living rather extravagantly in five-star hotels at beach casinos.

Adom was pulled over by the police, who opened the trunk of his car and seized two hay bales of marijuana, a shipment of cocaine from

Colombia shipped by Dunkin Colomon, and two hundred thousand dollars cash in hundred-dollar bills. Adom went up the river to Sing Sing for almost a year despite his family hiring the best lawyers. Luckily, he had still been technically a minor, or he would have received a fifteen-year sentence.

Duncan and Darcy moved back into the woods cold turkey, where many wild actual turkeys were roaming, this being New England. There, they met the Canoe Lady, a hippie redneck from the poorest state in the lower forty-eight states, Mississippi.

Canoe Lady had two dazzlingly beautiful daughters, Heather Lynn and Rebecca Rainbow Becky, and they all lived off the land, poaching deer and fishing for trout. They all swam naked in the Ham River in Easton Valley at Baby Beach, a favorite of Franconia college hippies and an unparalleled nudist beach. The police were afraid to go there; it was that disgusting.

Love, peace, hallucinogens, and draft evasion. In spite of it all, Heather Lynn decided on a military career with the US Navy intelligence because she was very blue-eyed, blonde, and Germanic like her sister, but more so—and smart as a whip to boot!

The US Navy hastily discharged her halfway through her career when it became obvious she had seen far too much classified information on everything sensitive and embarrassing to our government. She was now a threat to national security, and lo and behold, only a few months passed before she was run over and killed by a drunk driver in Mississippi, her home state, not too terribly far from Sugar Hill, New Hampshire.

Canoe Lady sued the family and the estate of the drunk driver and was awarded two hundred thousand dollars, but the money was no consolation for the loss of a genius, charming child who could easily have become the governor of any state. Canoe Lady, now thoroughly depressed, went to every major casino on the Mississippi and then Foxwoods Casino in Connecticut. She gambled away every last dime before the year had ended, but luckily her surviving daughter, Rebecca Rainbow Becky, had talked her into buying two acres in Bethlehem Hollow by the Ammonoosuc River from the ninety-year-old retired Pan-Am pilot Frederick Von Lederhosen, where they erected a teepee and then slowly added an entire collection of abandoned campers, giving it the appearance of an Indian encampment in Canada. But this wasn't Canada at all—this was deep, dark, mysterious Bethlehem Hollow, home of several hillbilly logger families who were possibly inbred because at one time they had chained Duncan Millar to a quadrocycle and then dragged him through the woods until possibly dead, burying him under a pile of leaves and then driving away.

Craig's Vietnam veteran friend Danny, who had served three tours, went over to that hillbilly house with his huge 9mm Magnum pistol with long silencer to give the irresponsible party a good talking to.

"Go ahead and give me some reason not to kill you. It's most likely inevitable With this gun stuck up your nostril, you may get a fleeting glimpses of your very own brains covering the ceiling above your fucking eyes. Have a good last look!"

Danny was one of those people on the Earth one didn't want as an enemy. These were all the Bethlehem Hollow boys, one of whom would date the newly arrived hippie in town, Fallon From Out Nowhere. They would like to ride motorcycles, skidders, or whatever. With short pieces of cut logging chain, they would whip the faces of nonbelievers, dislodging eyeballs and breaking jaws, skulls, and teeth. Even with all the spoiled city kids emigrating to the New Hampshire woods, there were still pockets of inbred, down-home hillbillies in backwoods sections of the state such as Dalton, home of the notorious drug-dealing Dalton Gang!

Roger and Debbie decided it would be okay if Myra, a girl from Honduras, could stay with them because Hillary was lonely. Myra attended high school in Littleton and amazingly learned to speak English. Duncan Millar saw his opportunity. He enticed her into the woods and pulled down her pants and his own. Her mouth opened wide after a few hits off the reefer joint. So Myra joined the rebellion too.

"Such a revolution, such a revolution!" Duncan Millar now had a new girlfriend, his sort-of stepsister. But love is love, and there is no time to waste in the United States because you might get drafted next week and be in the army next month in some faraway country, getting shot in the ass—or worse!

After a few happy years together, still being sponsored by liberal parents, they both moved to Concord, then Manchester, New Hampshire, where Myra worked as a cocktail waitress and became a nurse at the hospital. Duncan Millar had less glamorous jobs at a factory and then at another factory. Myra was indeed stepping up while Duncan Millar seemed to be going nowhere at all, going from one boring factory to the next. They separated ways.

Myra decided she had found her new old man, possibly to marry, because he was rich. He was the heroin dealer of Laconia on Lake Winnipesaukee. He had been living with his mother and brother at home but now decided to rent an upstairs flat with his hot new girlfriend from Honduras, Myra, who had spent her baby years crawling with siblings and cousins on a dirt floor under a thatched grass roof. Now she was an American living the life with her dealer. Now she had a candy man who could supply her daily habit of smack, and his supply was so large that she would never run out. He locked her in the apartment with all his drugs, unless he needed her as a runner-for a delivery somewhere!

Duncan Millar first got word of this on the street, and then later from text messages sent from Myra that she had been kidnapped, tortured, and beaten by her current lover, who broke into wild rages and tantrums while blaming her for all his misery. He would yell, scream, throw things, and then punch her in the face. He said if she were to leave, he would hunt her down and kill her.

Duncan Millar, who was now living with me, talked me into a rescue mission with my car. We would go to Laconia in the black of a cold winter evening and on the pretext of delivering her old clothing, a few trinkets, and jewelry. We would visit them, and she would be able to sneak out of the house and into my car. We sped away even though she had left behind everything she owned. We went down the highway and sped between snowbanks piled high from March spring snowfall. It was pitch-black, with not even a moon but some stars.

"Gotta get away, gotta get away!" The radio played a getaway song for our bold misadventure. We would hide Myra at our house for a while, knowing he would probably find us in a week or two.

THE AXMAN COMETH

THE **W**HILE OUT THE KITCHEN WINDOW, I DECIDE TO CALL OUT LOUD to Duncan Millar and Myra in the bedroom, still sleeping or screwing or whatever. "There's a strange-looking motherfucker in our driveway! Holy shit, looks like that strange son of a bitch from Laconia!"

Oh, my god, he has indeed found our location, and now it probably is his ambition to bring Myra back to their not-so-happy home—not a very good scenario. Maybe he has a gun?

Duncan Millar wakes up and suggests I go out there in the driveway and pay the visitor a few dollars to split some wood, keep him happy.

He begins swinging the axe in our driveway. *Blonk, blonk, blonk.*

Myra gathers her things, and she is out the door and going to return there to gather her clothes, then somehow escape again. Duncan Millar reassures me.

Two days later, she evidently pulls off her escapade to a girlfriend's house. Duncan Millar reassures me again that he has heard from her. Then he goes down to the gas station not too far from our house, gets his rack of beer and loads it into his backpack, and buys the *Manchester Union Leader*, the state's official newspaper because it has destroyed all competition.

"Myra's boyfriend has been detained by police in Laconia, pending an investigation of a double homicide involving his mother and brother," Millar announces.

"Oh, that's a bad neighborhood there, if it's some kind of drug war or something?" I reply.

"Both of them were hacked to death by a machete, with blood splattered everywhere," Millar reads. Then he adds, "The main suspect is now Myra's boyfriend because he was driving the mother's car we sold to her—that white Ford van."

Cindy is on her way over here this morning to spy on us, perhaps. Don't say anything about this to Cindy," I protest

Indeed, Cindy became Duncan Millar's official godmother at his birth thirty years ago. Then Cindy, while working as a receptionist at a very large and prominent Boston bank, fell in love with Burt Lack, who was making rather large deposits because he had sold his electronic company for twenty-seven million dollars. They were married three months later with her parents' approval.

Her father had given her a list of people to marry years before, and my name had not been included Well, now she is happy, and her spouse seemed puzzled when he saw me at the Village Store and asked me why I hadn't married her and saved him the trouble of marrying someone else's girlfriend. Hmm.

I hadn't married her because we were living at thirteen thousand feet in a tent eating crows, porcupines, marmots, and the like, living day to day and probably at too close quarters. Yes, we were a bit in each other's space and in each other's hair. Largely because we ran out of weed to smoke to deaden the pain of our suffering, we parted ways, and she went to the big city of Los Angeles for a year to finally have a career—as a lap dancer.

Luckily, that wasn't her life's ambition. But now thirty-two years later, she is coming over to our house (well. really my father's, because he bought it under her recommendation).

"She will send you to vocational institute to learn a trade when you stop drinking," I remind Duncan Millar of her empty promise. We both know he is Irish and will drink like a fish until the day he dies, probably in eleven years at age forty-one. Sad.

"If only your lesbian sister's girlfriend hadn't attacked you with that butcher's knife ten years ago," I theorize. It was that terrible event that hooked twenty-one-year-old Duncan Millar on oxycontin. Now, in order to get off his addiction to those twenty-five-dollar painkiller pills, there is a thirty-eight-dollar pill.

"Somebody's getting rich off all these pills, and it's not you and me!" I remind Duncan Millar, knowing full well it's that the daughter of the postmaster I dated forty years ago and is now a biochemist is probably also the VP of the oxycontin company.

"Well, it's now my livelihood—and Myra's too!" Millar responds. "It's the only employer out there in the streets. Everybody's on these pills by prescription, and everybody's selling them in the streets and getting rich!" Millar states a well-known modern fact. The truth.

Last summer alone, Duncan Millar picked up thirteen girlfriends by selling them his extra pills. Not too bad a tally for a summer, but he'll catch a disease or maybe knock one up, and then game over—he'll be changing diapers and working at the factory. I don't see what these girls see in him, but he is a nice guy with red hair, blue eyes, and plentiful prescriptions!

A year ago before I bought this house, we were both camping in the National Forest on Mt. Garfield. But now we are at home in my father's house that he bought with my grandfather's trust fund.

We had been scrounging in the streets like homeless dogs for each and every meal, but of course in Concord, New Hampshire, the state capital, there is The Friendly Kitchen, offering the homeless and hungry three square meals daily. What a rough crowd that had been, mostly just-out-of-jail people.

To celebrate my new success in life, I decided to vacation in Chile, where I picked up a homeless dog in the streets because we had a lot in common. Her name was … well, I called her Jovenita, young thing. She became simply Nita.

Duncan Millar and Myra were there at JFK Airport in New York when Nita came all the way from Chile via LAN Cargo, and Myra, who speaks Spanish, could read all the paperwork and claim our new pet sent from heaven.

Duncan Millar went walking the new dog down to the gas station, and he met his ex-girlfriend Stacy's cousin, Marlaya, whom he had met twice at Salisbury Port Beach years ago and always felt strongly for. Sure enough, Marlaya felt the same way even though she had no addictions, so she became pregnant, and now we are all waiting for the arrival of the baby next month.

I expect it's probably the Lord's work because we have all been converted and born again by Jehovah's witnesses that come to our door every other day and pray. We pray that this blood moon will not be the fourth and trigger the Apocalypse and Armageddon because we want to ski at least one more season.

We are just one big happy family now as brothers and sisters of God's kingdom here on Earth, though temporarily because we are all destined to live in heaven for sure.

Cindy's son has made the US ski team, and I have started figure skating on Streeter Pond every Sunday after church. Adom has been released from prison and is winning local beer league ski races at Cannon Mountain, although there is one slight setback: he crashed his motorcycle into a tree, breaking all his ribs. Oh, well; they will heal. Cindy hasn't filed for a divorce, and Roger is recovering from cancer and has found the Lord, to whom we are indebted for all our grace to liberate us from our worldly suffering.

KISSING ON THE SKI LIFT, AGE FOURTEEN

I suppose it really accelerated my ski career,

All those sweet young kisses on the ski lift with Penny Grisvold.

Later in my life, some woman described her:

"Penny, she's a tiny little thing."

She hardly ever seemed tiny to me because she was my big picture.

I rode the double lift with her at Mad River Glen in Vermont.

Those were slow lift rides back then in the 1960s;

Sometimes the lift broke down or ran very slow.

All the more time for passing Lifesavers or chewing gum.

She wore hot red lipstick, or sometimes pink.

No one could see us up there between the trees.

All the other children skiing below, sometimes singing,

"Duncan and Penny up in a tree, K-I-S-S-I-N-G."

My ski coach wanted me to spend more time doing parallel turns down the fall line, planting my ski poles,

Not chasing girls.

"That comes soon enough, marriage and babies. Keep skiing!" he warned me with his thick Austrian accent.

Howdy Howard Munn and Rosi Fortna were my competition for his approval.

Howdy had to go milk cows before and after every ski practice, so he was tired.

Rosi had been wandering around Naples, Italy, after the war in her diapers.

Rumor had it her parents died in a car crash, so she was adopted by an American family, Lixi Todd Fortna, a Sugarbush ski instructor.

Penny could not ski to save her own life and did an advanced snowplow.

Rosi could ski circles around me in glades and in moguls.

I would keep trying, I would keep trying. All those kisses

Made me ski faster, made me go faster down the big snow and ice-covered mountain.

EVACUATION AT PORTILLO, 1965

T IS ALWAYS A GOOD YEAR WHEN YOU ARE A SEVENTEEN-YEAR-OLD BECAUSE your fresh, new life is exciting with each new day full of adventure. It is good to be alive and have somewhere new to go and something new to see. When you are a child, every dessert is a delight, and when you are a seventeen-year-old male, the girls have suddenly become young women with wavy hair and bright beaming eyes, expecting adventure from you.

I had been in so much trouble as a sixteen-year-old and was unsure exactly what caused such a messy year in my life. Would my own father forgive me my trespasses and allow me back in Portillo, Chile?

My governess, Caroline, spoke wisely. "If you are going to ask your father if you may go to South America, this is not a good week to ask him because he is in a very bad mood due to the stock market. I'll let you know when he will be in a good mood so that you will get a positive result!" Caroline was very wise and found the optimum time for me to pop the question.

A frown came on his face for about fifteen seconds but then went away, and he wanted me to be sure that my request was genuine. "Did Caroline ask you to ask me about this? They have plans to go to England and see their relatives—if, of course, they won't be needed here to babysit you all summer."

I had been living with the French family all winter long on skiing weekends and had competed and won at the US Junior National Ski Championships. However, it was decided that I should return to my father's house for the duration of the summer, where my stepmother, Dorothy was far less enthusiastic about my return. She said to my father, "Darling, my children are now your dear children, and this extra one from your ill first wife is equally as ill. What can be done with him?"

He told me, "Yes, I'll arrange with my secretary, Mildred, to purchase an airline ticket for you for three weeks, or—"

"Six weeks, please, Father!"

"Okay," he relented, smiling because he knew this would be great news to my stepmother.

There was sibling rivalry at the French home, and my former friend, upon becoming my almost brother, had turned against me. Plus, their daughter, Janice, wanted more time alone with her overworked mother, Hope. My former home was no longer waiting with open arms for me. I boarded the Pan American Airways turboprop with stops in Miami, Panama, and Lima before it landed in Santiago, which means St. James, but that could hardly concern me because at seventeen, I was no angel in waiting.

Then the long, slow cog train from Los Andes to Portillo. I had been waiting for it the year before when the owner at my hotel had said, "There are really bad people looking for you. Go with my Syrian sons to the Statue of Jesus; they won't be looking for you there." But all of that year was mostly washed from my mind now because of electric shock treatment. It was as though I had been born all over again at seventeen, minus a few recent years, so I was thinking more like a twelve-year-old.

The train climbed slowly through the barren Andean Valley to Rio Blanco (White River), a tiny hamlet where children ran barefoot through a few inches of freshly fallen snow. The Chilean peasants had nothing but rags to wear, but they wore huge smiles upon seeing the daily train, which in that smallest dot on the planet was like the Queen Mary entering New York Harbor.

I piled my clothes and ski boots in the small closet in my bunk room in the Grand Hotel "Portillo," a little port on the lake of the Inca, whose princess, fleeing from the Spanish Conquistadors, preferred to drown there rather than be captured. Hundreds of years had passed since then.

Now it became an opulent resort, a jewel in the Andes Mountains of Chile.

I had the Reese brothers for roommates, but one, Jerry, would be leaving for the Rotunda, a big, circular rock house down by the ski lift that housed the ski patrol, which he would join. Rig wanted to be one also but was considered too young, like me. There wasn't a whole lot to do in Portillo in 1965, which had one telephone or maybe three, but they were linked by lines crossed by avalanches. Luckily, I had brought my chess set with me but now had to find someone who enjoyed the game down in the hotel living room.

I was in luck because there was a twenty-year-old Cornell University student named Ronald "Ron" Hock who was playing chess against himself with a clock. I would never present any great challenge to him, only beating him once when he lost his queen. He knew every possible opening and every defense—the Sicilian Defense, the Queen's Gambit, and so on. He often opened up knight's pawn to K3. Then he moved his bishops out in front of each rook. He would create a crossfire at the center of the chessboard. I had never seen anything like it; my father and Othmar Schneider, the ski school director, would sometimes play maybe one bishop in such a manner, but rarely both.

Ron was from New York and was no great skier or athlete, but he was a city boy, so his parents must have felt compelled to send him out into the world of adventure to become a man, get out of mother's hair, and do more than just errands with the house servants all summer. His parents must have had adventure plans of their own. We played a lot of chess every evening for almost two weeks. There was a massive storm brewing in the Pacific somewhere, and it was expected to hit central Chile and give Portillo possibly five feet of snow. Ron wanted to be on the ski patrol like Jerry Reese, and he was waiting for his application to be reviewed by Henry Purcell, the owner, and Othmar Schneider, the director of everything on snow, including the ski school and the ski patrol. Othmar had won the 1952 Olympic slalom, narrowly beating Stein Erikson, the Norwegian.

Othmar summoned me and said that my skiing was not improving and that I was wasting my time imitating Willy Bogner and Fritz Wagnerberger, both German downhillers who did some strange counterrotation windup before each turn, whereas the Austrians always faced downhill.

Then good news came, and Ron beamed with excitement because he was hired by the ski patrol and would be packing up all his things to move to the Rotunda. The wind was blowing sixty miles per hour, and the ski lifts shut early because the chairs were almost swinging into the chairlift towers supporting the cables. It began to snow like hell, and the wind was almost deafening.

"This is a very big and dangerous storm, and we are asking everyone to stay indoors for two days, possibly three, until the wind subsides," announced Othmar with Henry Purcell standing behind him. The electric lights were flickering in the hotel and then went out. Some candles and some lanterns were lit.

The snow was piling up, and someone said, "Over eight feet deep already." There was no one to play chess with now, and even the Chilean Army ski troops had retreated into their housing a mile distant in the grayout. It was all gray outside with swirling snow, so I went to bed and slept a deep sleep until I heard the yelling

"Help, help, help!"

It was coming from outside and three stories below. I could hear some window shutters banging open, possibly from Othmar and Uka's room. (He had a Chilean mistress.)

Then there was a banging on the metal doors below, and I could barely hear the loud cry. "Avalancha!" Chilean for *avalanche*. We sat up in our bunks and wondered what new excitement this storm must have brought with it. I decided to get dressed and go downstairs. Men were passing out shovels. I took one, and they said, yes, I would need my skis. It was now becoming visibly white outdoors; night had ended. The near naked man who had been yelling had crawled from the rotunda. Possibly it was Dick Hawkins—or was it Jerry Reese?

I made my way to the lower side of the rotunda, where there was a backdoor a soldier had opened. I looked up the staircase. It was full of snow and dripping water from broken pipes. I began shoveling upward. Finally someone said, "He's too young—get him out of here," pointing to me. It was very tall Victor of the ski school. I was exhausted by now anyway, so I left the stairwell and went back outside as a dozen

Chilean soldiers came inside to replace me. I climbed up the twisted avalanche icy debris to the other side of the building, where the snow was thirty feet higher. An avalanche possibly forty feet deep in a valley had accumulated from a scree field beneath two thousand feet of sheer cliffs, up against which the fierce, unyielding wind had piled a mile-wide snow drift. It had sheared and broken off to cause this destruction. A stone house had withstood most of the blow, but the roof had been blown off by the two-hundred-mile-per-hour wind preceding the avalanche. The ski patrollers in the upper bunks were missing. Ron had been the last hired, and the upper bunks were available because the lower bunks were cherished by the veteran patrollers.

I stood exhausted on the packed avalanche until ordered to leave the premises. Where I had stood, suddenly an arm popped through the snow. They dug them all out, still alive but terribly cold, and loaded them on toboggans, bringing them up to the hotel one by one. They all cried almost in unison, "I don't want to die. I don't want to die!"

Once inside, where their chilled bodies could warm, each one hemorrhaged, and each one died. They had been crushed internally by the densely packed avalanche snow, which was more like solid ice.

I had lost a friend. Jerry Reese had been on the bunk below as has Dick Hawkins. At first people thought that this must be some kind of nightmare. But they pushed up through the snow and felt the bottom of the upper bunk. They were lucky and lived.

I disobeyed orders and broke into the infirmary later that night. There they were, cold and pale corpses, some with eyes still open. Five of them at least.

We were ordered to evacuate Portillo because there was no more food, and the railroad was cut off by fifteen avalanches. I disobeyed orders again and rushed to the front ahead of our Austrian ski school–certified guides, who kept exclaiming, "Wait for us, wait! There might be another avalanche!"

I was to be chaperoned by the Ernst Engel family, which had two attractive daughters who were still minors. We went to La Parva a nearby ski area, to Santiago, where I was summoned by Mrs. Engel to play Bridge because they needed a fourth partner.

"What if I want to ski, go climb up the hill?"

"I'll have you arrested. You are a minor—do as I say!" was her stern reply. Very Austrian. I was to forget skiing for the entire week; possibly I had been traumatized?

RIP, Ron Hock from Cornell University. Why did God take you?

EDUCATION

Education is a personal choice.

How good it is to have a friend!

Now we know twice as much as I myself alone,

And especially an older friend who is wise,

Seasoned by many years yet well,

Healthy as though saved by some morality.

Good habits are like a strong back brace.

Those who continue to survive have learned the natural laws.

Our common code of behavior when dealing with others …

We cling to righteousness and to those who are just.

Our friends treat us with respect and dignity.

Our bodies are our temples, and our minds

Are mostly filled with fond memories

Of dear friends, some no longer living

But living in us, in our dearest chapel,

The human mind a friend and steward of our planet.

My best friend, my mind, I treat with respect and remain sober and alert

To the winds of change, to our new surroundings.

We move forward in time but look both ways,

Back at memories of friends, but forward

To new friends who rise on our horizon.

Like the sun itself, like planets in space, like new dancers on the grandest stage!

(School is now any environment where you find friends, the center that bears responsibility for the safety of all is our teacher, rabbi.)

FRANNY ON MOUNT EVEREST

LET US REMEMBER THAT IT WAS THE INTENSITY WITH WHICH WE LIVED and be remembered for that rather than for longevity. All of the preceding because life is but five deep breaths, not more.

We are like the grass that grows before noon and wilts all too soon when the sun does zenith overhead.

Franny was my friend who perhaps loved more my dog Helga than me at first. She invited us over for dinner, being delighted to cook something delicious for my dear dog Helga, who took a very kind fancy to all females because they were her own sex.

Franny had been raised in Columbia, Missouri, which is a slightly northern outpost of Dixie between Kansas City and St. Louis. Her father was a professor there at the University of Missouri. I had gone there once in my younger days to be turned down in love by a beautiful young blonde actress with very Saxon features.

Now, being older and wiser, though reeling in pain and suffering from a sudden divorce with children, I had started a new job as ski instructor in the prestigious western ski resort, Telluride, Colorado.

Franny asked me exactly how I made love, which was puzzling to her because her boss, Johnny Stevens, had informed her that I must be gay. I began to try to explain, but it was no use and much easier to follow her leads and not contradict her in any way, and soon I was rubbing her back for her after the very pleasant dinner with some wine.

She had no objections nor any fear of me, a gay man understandably. Her buttocks, which cried out for attention and massage, were perhaps the most amazing I had ever encountered—bonny hot crossed buns, indeed. She had climbed Mount Kendall, 13,455 feet high, in nearby Silverton in an hour and twenty minutes, setting a new record for that competition every summer. I doubt anyone has since broken it.

Her passion, aside from skiing, was evidently hiking high up the sides of the Rocky Mountains and other lofty mountains. Soon she would travel to Russia to climb Mt. Stalin, which has been renamed something else but is still the same height, 25,091 feet. There, she would fall in love with her guide, the Russian climber Antsiuev, whose partner the previous year had perished on Mount Everest guiding too many inexperienced climbers up there to their deaths for a great sum of money he would not live to spend.

Franny and Antsiev married, and he built her a house near Telluride, which they then mortgaged to finance their climbing adventure up Mount Everest. At the last minute, she invited me to her new home, perhaps to see them off or perhaps because she not only loved her new husband but feared him as well. Unfortunately, I declined, being both busy and absurdly jealous. Off they traveled in spite of her small son's nightmare that they would be lost in a snowstorm on top of a very high mountain.

I was in a breakfast cafe in Glenwood Springs, Colorado, a few months later while my dog Helga patiently waited for me in the car outside for all the best scraps I might bring her.

There was some news on the television about an American hiker who had just climbed Mount Everest without oxygen and had been the very first woman ever to do that, and her name was something strange, some Russian-sounding name. Unfortunately, she and her husband had tried to set up their tent on the descent in hundred-mile-per-hour winds, but it had been blown away, so they continued down by foot too rapidly to the twenty-thousand-foot level. She had gotten the bends, so he wandered off to find help. They had been up there above sixteen thousand feet for over a month, acclimatizing so as to make an ascent without oxygen.

Unfortunately, she was found near death, and he went insane and wandered off somewhere, perhaps disappearing into a crevasse.

I had heard enough and I rushed to buy a newspaper or two. I discovered to my horror and disappointment that it was indeed my Franny, my teammate in the Telluride Governor's Cup ski competition, which our team, including Colorado's own Governor Romer, had won the year before. (I had beaten Franz Klammer by 0.1 seconds for fastest time.)

I went to the memorial service held for her. Her first husband and young son were in attendance, and we all cried many tears for her and maybe ourselves as well.

Years passed by, and many more of my friends and former ladies of renown have likewise passed as well. Let us remember them dearly—not how they all died, but how each one lived exuberantly and passionately. They sprang up before us like shining flowers in a sunlit field in splendid colors, each one given exceptional beauty and grace by God alone.

I want to thank God also for my own life, which has been blessed meeting so many very special gifted people. Each person had a very important impact on my own life, as ordained by our Lord and Creator, to bring great joy into this world.

It shall not matter that we face world wars or pandemics threatening us with gloom and doom, because we are all shining flowers like Franny Each and every one of us is very special to God in both this life and hereafter.

There is great adversity in this world and suffering. It is there in order for us to not be spineless wimps but courageous heroes, because that is what God wants for us—that we each reach our great summit like Franny on Mount Everest. Thank you, God, for creating Franny to show us the way up, the way up there to that lofty summit of your grace and eternal love for us, so that we may now love each other more deeply.

Franny was barely alive when some American climbers said they stumbled upon her, and she said, "I'm an American. Can you help me?"

A storm was coming in, and the climbers had to abandon her, they said. Seven years later, they returned because of their conscience to find her still there, frozen in the snow with a smile on her face. They called her Sleeping Beauty when they had first found her seven years before.

Now, they pulled her body into a more remote location and draped an American flag over her, held down by some rocks. Franny is still there on Mount Everest.

IN THE LAND
OF THE TURTLE
(IN THE LATER YEARS,
IN THE LATTER YEARS)

In the later years of your own life,

I might reveal myself to you.

I might reveal what is in my sacred heart:

That who I am, you may be also.

Because you love me now that you shall know me,

That it is I who loves you so.

You were thinking that he loves me or he loves me not.

In your flippant youth, you were looking for a man

Who might love you truly and lead you by the hand

Down the aisle of your church, but it is really my church.

I have been with you from your very first day,

And I will be with you until the very end of time.

You are faithful to me, O daughters of Jerusalem.

I have prepared a groom for you in my image.

You will consider that he is a saint, at least in your eyes and ears.

His scent will be wonderful like myrrh and sage.

Your nostrils shall flare like the best of Arabian stallions.

I will send a magic carpet for you to ride; in your dreams, you will fly high.

Like eagles above, you will soar, even to the high peaks,

To look for me, your beloved, the one who shall kneel with you under my cherry tree,

Under an apple tree, where you were born. The birds flew to your window

To marvel at your beauty, and now he comes for you your beloved.

Like a stag upon the hills, he runs into your life to make it whole and complete.

You are blessed among women, O daughters of Jerusalem.

A groom is coming from Shiloh and from Mitzvah,

Someone who shall be with you into your latter years a husband and a father.

So dress up accordingly and walk with your sisters

That you might be seen in the land of the turtle,

Where the hummingbirds fly to their nests in the land of the living.

My anointed live there, where fresh breezes kiss the hilltops.

On my blessed hill, it is no insurmountable mountain.

There are many trees, and there are many hills.

Many pathways are there, and gentle roads that rise up beneath your feet.

You will walk and search for the one who loves you.

It is I.

It is I who loves you, and it is I who you were born to love.

Do not tarry long, do not hesitate to look for me.

I am here, I am there, and I am everywhere.

You will see me, you will behold my face, and I yours.

Even in the latter days, when I shall still love you even more,

Even then shall you love me and reminisce how you loved me always.

From the beginning you knew it was me; you called my name.

You wrote me a letter, you called me, and I came running to be with you

To be by your side and walk on this pathway to these falls, where we swim

In our beloved garden, which is this Earth also.

So tell your daughters and your sons to be careful with this Earth,

This Earth I created for you in your paradise here and now.

Think of me often think that I am still with you.

I never died, I never left you; I am a spirit indestructible.

I am with you always; just call my name, and I shall answer.

I am the wind in your hair, your sun and moon.

I make the clouds to refresh you; I am the morning mist.

Every fresh drink of cool water that you drink, I kiss your lips.

I am here forever, like a saint; you shall remember my love for you.

O daughter of Jerusalem, you are blessed on these sugar hills

We did walk together. I held your hand. Remember me.

THE GREAT
HEBREW (JEW)

The Great Hebrew

Anyone who studies the Bible diligently is likened to a great Hebrew.

A bookworm and a scribe is one who quotes Jesus, and of course

All the prophets who predicted the Messiah were all great Hebrews as well.

Money only makes the money lender and does not make the Hebrew

Because the Hebrew is like Abraham, a man of faith who believes in God,

Who believes in God and everything God has said through his prophets,

Who believes that Jesus was a rabbi, which means teacher.

Sent into this world created by God, both the world and the teacher,

To instruct those whose ears are willing to hear the truth and love as well

Every peacemaker as well as the peace that dwells within us.

When we turn to God for our salvation, it is apparent we cannot save ourselves,

So the great Hebrew came into this world to save us with scripture

That protruded from his mouth like a sharp sword.

His raiment of love is like a beacon of light to lost ships on the sea.

He is someone who does not demand your servitude, but you serve his every need.

What he needs most is you, his student; otherwise he is no purpose.

So he finds you, or you find him, and you cannot turn away because you

Are starving for all his knowledge, everything he knows, his every word.

You mumble upon your lips all he has said and done is worth remembering.

When he is led away, you protest, you wonder, How can this be,

That God brought a great man into your life to counsel you?

Why would God take this man away from you? You meditate, you wonder.

Why are you so sad, and what is this you have written down about that man?

Perhaps it is a textbook, or maybe it is a story you will tell.

Younger people now crowd about you to hear what you might tell them.

You speak of love and devotion and commitment to a cause.

You say we are all members of the same team, which is our community or puebla.

Everyone must serve a master, and you have chosen God, who is gracious.

God, who shows mercy and forgiveness. God, who heals our wounds and broken hearts.

He leads us beside still waters that refresh us. He shines a light for us in the darkness.

We are all his people, and he is our God, the Father of Abraham.

He is the great scholar, our God in heaven, who loves us and has written every loving word

HUMPTY IN HIS LIMO

I am here to fulfill the prophecies of our Lord and Creator.

Let my name be added to this book of life that I might live.

Take away this pestilence from me that I might breathe and walk

Among my friends, for each one is a saint sent by you God.

Every enemy is a tool of St. Adversity to purify me like gold.

If my friends consider themselves to be as enemies, such is life.

What have I done to offend them? Did I lie to them? I think not.

A liar is his own enemy; he creates a web of deceit but deceives himself.

What will he do on the day of reckoning, when God shall call his bluff?

He holds the joker and a few low cards up his sleeves.

He imagines that all the money on the table is his, but guess again.

Don't be a loser in life. Walk tall and be proud of yourself and your flag.

God has given you a banner to hold high on this battlefield for righteousness.

If the enemy does not believe in God, he will be vanquished.

It is written that the sons of perdition shall be trampled in a great wine press.

All their blood is the fertilizer of this Earth; thereby the crops grow tall.

So who are you to contest what the Lord has decreed in holy verse?

In the book of life, there is death for that villain who deceives the unfaithful.

You would imagine falsely that you would not be fooled; you think you are smart.

You read the *New York Times* or *Pravda* and believe what the experts tell you.

You make wise investments but do not invest to help your own family members.

You have forsaken the cries of the poor, the widowed, and the imprisoned

To live a life on your property surrounded by high walls and dogs.

At least you have those dogs for friends, but if you are a demon, your own dogs will bite you.

They are hungry for the ass of a swine like you, a giant ham.

You think this is all funny that you inherit riches and make great investments.

You are amused by the news of the day, plagues, wars, and refugees who are homeless.

There you sit in your mansion with your giant television in HD and three dimensions.

Now, get your laptop and buy more furniture and more clothes and more jewelry.

It will take a lot of makeup and hair spray to disguise your greed.

God is most ashamed of those who are not charitable.

So when your friends ask for money, give something and at least toss some coins to street beggars.

There are many homeless now; this is like the Great Depression, and many are sick and poor

While you in your limousine go kingdom driving to prove you are above it all.

You are lofty, you have deceived yourself, you drive drunk, you lose control.

Now you are in front of the judge, but you have the very best lawyer.

The doctors have pinned your broken arm, but it is what is in your head that's infirmed.

You dreamed of being a big shot wrapped in minks with a big hat, like some drug dealer.

You entered the stage to give your grand speech to announce your candidacy.

People are clapping; you have told them that it is all right to be greedy and self-centered.

You will help their stock portfolios. You will end this great recession and lower interest rates.

You are their Messiah, and you are on television each and every day.

However, the pestilence and pandemic is worsening; all the news is foreboding.

You are a great Humpty Dumpty on your high wall; you shall indeed fall.

All the king's horses and all the king's men will refuse to put you back together again.

"Next, next, next!" they cry in all the marketplaces of the world.

It is another sad scenario: all that goes up must come down.

Build for yourself some treasures in heaven, not just the Earth.

Love one another and rejoice that you can help your needy neighbor.

You really don't want to end up like that guy on television; everyone pays him lip service,

Yet when he falls, all the king's horses and men ride away laughing.

Your needy neighbor is not laughing at you and will remember every penny.

Give of yourself. Give because God is watching, as are all the angels.

EVERY MAN IS JESUS

Every man is Jesus,
Because he must die
And therefore face the truth
On love, indeed love, indeed that great Judgment Day,
When all that shall burn pure
Will be left, only the love of God the Father.
Every man's love indeed
Shall return to God in that moment,
And Jesus, who reigns inside
Deep in the core of every man living,
Shall reign supreme.
And everyone else
Shall burn up in the flames.
The hot, naked truth:
Only our love shall survive.
Every other emotion
Shall have gone to hell.
So why waste your precious time
On anything short of love?
All of it shall be subtracted;
Only love shall be an addition
To your precious life.
If it is precious to you at all,
Go on living, go on loving everything else fall by the wayside.
Be added unto the kingdom of God.

Let everything else fall by the wayside; everything else will not
withstand the fire and heat
Of God's love, only love itself,
More precious than gold.
And the Word of God
Shall endure forever
Because it is written
You shall love the lord your God,
And you shall love your neighbor
As much as yourself, or be cast into hell and the pit.
So why suffer shame and rejection?
You have already suffered a lifetime in the flesh.
The flesh is not immortal,
But the spirit can be,
Connected by love
To the greatest of spirits.
For God so loved the world,
He gave His only Son
That man might be redeemed, every man
From his fall from Paradise
Into the earthly death trap.
Waste your short time no more.
You are but a fleeting shadow upon the earth.
A brief flame, you rise up then perish like the grass.
Your life is only a number of days.
There is no escaping.
Bow down before your Maker.
Kneel upon your pew.
Confess your inadequacy and shortcoming.
Return to the God, who loves you!

A MAN ON A
CAMEL, PART 7

HERE WE ARE AGAIN, BEARING WITNESS OF THIS MAN ON A CAMEL trotting across the desert. The camel can go quite some distance without stopping to drink water. The man has a canteen. He imagines he is a Mongolian riding a horse across the grasslands of Asia. He might cut the horse's neck with the point of a knife to drink its blood and avoid having to stop to prepare food. That is what the Mongols did: ride all night long behind enemy lines to set barns and stockpiles of food on fire, and terrorize the Europeans still fighting in heavy armor. The Mongols had cannons and rockets and guns. *Bang, bang, bang,* and then the Mongols had howitzers and mortars.

"There is no way I would drink my camel's blood!" thinks the man, who has befriended the camel, his only friend. They are in the middle of nowhere, a vast desert on a starry night. It is too hot to ride during the day—120 degrees or more. Their blood might boil. It would be the end of them both. Vultures would eat their remains after the jackals were done. Then some ants might finish off what is left. "Not very pretty at all, unless you are an ant," thinks the man. The camel is not thinking. He is trotting.

The man remembers when he was a young cadet in a military academy. War had broken out in a faraway province, Algeria. He was sent with his unit there in Algeria, where he took a bullet in his ass. It still hurts there a little. There is a slight scar where the army surgeon cut into him with the scalpel.

How he would like to return to Paris and drink coffee there, where the cars race by and one can see the Eiffel Tower. The young ladies dressed in the best Paris fashion with Easter bonnets, smiling in front of him and teasing everyone with such vibrancy.

Now he has miles to go, maybe just a thousand to Cairo. Perhaps this is too ambitious a plan to travel so far. He is a very long way from home with his new best friend, a camel. It spits and drools and has moments of insurrection. It is in part a wild beast but has a mind of its own.

Across the wasteland he rides, up to a place where there are rusty, metallic-looking trucks and tanks. This must be all that's left of Rommel's Afrika Korps. Maybe these are British. Everyone died here and there and over here. It's a cemetery of war. No one lives to tell about it. The stories are so ghastly that no one wants to remember. Forget the war. Forget that you too fought here and there, and those ones you met who died. Too bad for them. You would rather not remember that your comrades died here and there. Everywhere. A bullet hit this one, then that one.

It is time to ride away, far away, and forget all that. The man will finally sleep under the stars because he is so exhausted from so many memories. He has the reins of the camel so that no thief will sneak up and steal it away. That would be unthinkable, to be left out here in this vast expanse with no transportation. His feet would burn on the sand. His shoes would burn off his feet in one hundred miles. His feet would catch fire on the sand while buzzards cackled from all too nearby. He must not think like this. He must get some sleep, but not more than just a few hours. He must be up and gone before the sunrise, while it's still cool, before the sun gets up very far. By ten o'clock, the heat will be unbearable. Maybe he can find a shade tree. He will lie beneath the tree when he finds it, and the camel might even kneel to conserve water. Every drop of moisture evaporates. It is parching his throat again. He will drink another sip of water but be sparing because he hasn't yet found the oasis on the map. He has a trident and looks up into the stars to calculate where they must be. How did night come so fast? He has overslept again. What day is this? They all seem to merge into one day and one night. He has lost track of the time. His watch has stopped. He must find water. He must find water.

His life is not unlike your own. His life is not unlike your own. You are in a desert.

You must find God before you burn up in the heat. God has promised you the very water of life ...

MAN ON A CAMEL, PART 2

GOD WILL TELL ME WHAT TO WRITE.

A man on a camel, while crossing the desert, arrives at a lonely house in the middle of nowhere. There is a lone tree near the abandoned driveway. No one has been here for months, maybe years. Whose house could this be?

The door is open, so the man looks in. There is no furniture, but the entryway has a worn-out rug that says, "Welcome, stranger!"

The man goes into the house one step at a time. Who could have lived here in the middle of nowhere?

On the wall there is a painting of a sign. It says, "God dwells here with us!"

Very interesting, this is. Religious, pious people may have lived here—maybe Mormons or Quakers?

There is a refrigerator. The man opens it. "Help yourself" says a note. There is a glass of cold milk and some cookies.

"This must be some kind of joke," says the man.

"No joke at all," replies a voice from somewhere in the house. The man jumps from fright. Someone is here, but it must be someone he cannot see. He looks outside the windows. His camel is gone. Has someone ridden off on it? Had there been some other stranger hiding in a bedroom or closet?

The man runs out the door and into the blazing sun. The wind is blowing hard now. Perhaps a sandstorm is coming. He will have to take refuge in the house. He goes back inside. His camel is in the living room. Is there another door somewhere? He cannot locate it. The house has endless rooms. He now looks into one room, then the next.

What he has brought to this house is himself and the camel. Wherever you go, there you are, as they say.

If the man is a happy man who wanders here, he will remain happy. If he is a miserable man, he will stay miserable. The house is heaven, where you will spend at least one thousand years. Have you been good? Because goodness will make you happy. Have you behaved badly? Because now you will be a miserable wretch. You don't quite agree? Neither does God agree with you if you are unjust. You will be banished from all society and from the friendly angels if you are unfriendly and antisocial. Everything you do in this life will determine where you will arrive on that day. On that day of terrible judgment when the sand storm comes, will you find shelter and peace?

MAN ON A CAMEL, PART 5

A MAN IS CROSSING THE DESERT ON A CAMEL.
"I am doing this because God wills it!" he reasons.

He arrives in a small Mexican pueblita (little town), where there is a cantina, a bar and watering hole to fill one's canteen. Some people come running out its door before he enters. There is a fight ensuing and a lot of noise, like breaking chairs and glass bottles. Finally the combatants bring their fight into the street.

"Look at that stranger!" someone exclaims.

The men stop fighting and chase our man on his camel back out of town, throwing rocks and cursing.

"What a badass pueblito!" thinks our man on his camel, both of them now running for their lives into the desert. People who had hated one another, when threatened by any invader, suddenly became friends and allies to gang up on the newcomer.

Our man on his camel then arrives at another town, where there is a pandemic.

"Are you a doctor?" a desperate woman asks him.

"Well, yes, I am a homeopath, yes!" says our man, dismounting his camel. They follow the woman to a makeshift hospital in a tent. There are a lot of sick patients, all wearing masks on cots, with nurses in hazmat suits attending their every need.

"These people are not sick," says our man. "They are starving for this love given to them now by these nurses. If they had been loved at home, this disease would not have progressed so rapidly. This is not just a pandemic—it is a collection of very lost souls at a church 'dinner bell' free evening meal. They feign that they are hungry, but actually it's love they are starving for!"

"What a homeopath!" exclaims one nearby nurse, whose patient is now sitting up to listen to our man.

"God is here in the form of a prophet!" says another patient, sitting up to stare at the camel in the doorway drinking a bucket of water.

Our man wakes up under his camel, who is standing on top of him to shield him from the hot sun. He was dreaming again after falling off the camel from exhaustion. Night is coming, and it will cool off enough for him to regain his bearings and look for some water hole here in this vast desert. What he is really looking for is a woman who might resemble his own mother, a woman who has more to offer than just water and a pat on the back. She will have her own camel, and they will ride off together to be homeopaths and preach to the lost and sick.

"We come in the name of love. We come to free you from this disease of loneliness and desperation. You were lost, but now you are found. Love is here, entering your streets. The pandemic will end because you will rise up off your cots and hate each other no more, but become friends and allies!"

The sick get up off their beds and grab rocks and begin to pelt the man and his wife, who ride off quickly. Now the people are united. Now the people love each other again and hate the virus. Now those who were held captive by hatred show compassion for one another.

The man on his camel crosses the desert. Now he has a wife for a companion.

DEAR SARS·COV·2

Dear SARS-CoV-2, everyone says you are the enemy.

All of humankind, we eschew, profess our innocence.

The life of every mammal is endangered by global warming.

Somehow it is not our own fault, so now we have this new enemy.

Saint SARS-CoV-2, who has done more to slow global warming

Than any living US senator, this Saint Virus sent by our Creator,

Who has created everything, and everyone must be in disagreement with all our feigned innocence.

Our Creator has created something whereby we will possibly avoid total self-destruction.

Whereas we once burned fossil fuel like there would be no tomorrow,

Tomorrow is here now, and it's a brave new world indeed.

Hazmat suits and facemasks—we all look like space creatures.

Perhaps we are. Perhaps we are just very fortunate visitors here on this Earth.

We are possibly not its best stewards. We have, by our greed and lust,

Overconsumed everything in sight from Brazilian rainforest to swordfish and buffalo.

So by grace we are humbled once more, we learn only in our defeat.

We had been arrogant and haughty, led by greedy rich men with large stock portfolios

Who thought it funny that our oceans have become swirling garbage dumps of plastic.

It has not deterred them from driving Mercedes-Benzes and Alfa Romeos.

So Saint Virus, do as God shall command thee. Surely you serve his divine purpose reality.

Let us not fool ourselves—we are the main fools ourselves who have polluted everything and everywhere.

Yes, I have a very good life. Thank you, God, for everything you have done each and every day.

Dear SARS-CoV-2, you are a saint to take on humanity's greed and corruption,

Humanity's disregard and disrespect for all of this, one holy creation of one holy Creator.

MORE OF JIMMY ON
THE MOUNTAIN

"ANY DAY YOU CAN WAKE UP IN **A**MERICA AND MAKE A CUP OF coffee, even if you have no money at all, is a very good day indeed!" That was what Jimmy Thompson always said with a wide grin. Sometimes he would roll a joint, and we would smoke one or two puffs of that stuff too. Then he would extinguish it and save what was left for just before he went to sleep.

He did have nightmares and would wake up screaming, thinking he was back there in Nam, in that battle that almost ended his life. A great big guy, his friend, took a bullet or two and fell on top of him dead. It saved his life, at least, for that very moment when the battle broke out. The 101st had walked into a horseshoe-shaped ambush with the North Vietnamese regulars (NVRs) coming out of holes in the ground to catch the Americans in a deadly crossfire. Somehow, perhaps when darkness ensued, Jimmy managed to crawl under a tree that had been hit by a mortar, so of course there was no tree left but a big, dislodged root system with a hole under it. He continued to play dead. Only one other American was still alive in his vicinity, and they could hear the NVR doing a body count of the Americans, shooting anyone who was still alive. First light ensued, and those NVRs in their pajamas were getting really close, so they had to start shooting their very last magazines.

Luckily, at that moment US Navy Warthogs swooped down and dropped napalm, narrowly missing them. There were the screams of those being roasted in burning plastic, and the NVR who were still alive ran away.

Jimmy was medevaced by helicopter because his wounds were severe. He woke up in a hospital ship and then was flown back to the United States, where he gave some lectures to green recruits about to be shipped out to Nam. At least he now had hot coffee. After two months of this, despite being constantly recruited to re-up, he fought off the temptation, which for him was not so tempting at all. He had almost been killed, and everyone in his platoon of over one hundred had been killed except for seven of them. He felt very good to be alive. He relished every good cup of hot coffee, even if there was no cream or sugar.

He was discharged and returned to his mother Rita's house in North Conway, New Hampshire. One could get there by bus from Boston in about five hours back then. Coming back to placid little New Hampshire was like returning to Fairy Land or Walt Disney World. People he met in the streets were mostly war protestors, and very few thanked him for his service. These people, whether they were for or against the war, had almost no concept of total war other than *Hogan's Heroes* or *Gomer Pyle, U.S.M.C.* There were still some documentaries of Iwo Jima from World War II with the marines using flamethrowers and scalding everyone, but until you can smell burning flesh and possibly your own, you don't have any idea that you are totally expendable. The US military industrial complex wants you for cannon fodder.

Jimmy; his young wife, Cindy; and their daughter, Valerie, headed for Taos, New Mexico, to live with the Indians. Many of those Indians had served in various wars because it was their opportunity to get jobs and see the world, plus they would receive the GI Bill. A few even went to college, where they studied mostly agriculture or forestry. A few became lawyers and politicians. All the money in New Mexico was the Bank of Texas, which managed to buy most of the farms in eastern New Mexico, leaving just the badlands and some hills in western New Mexico to the Spanish or Indians, who intermarried. All the pure Indians—Navahos, Commanche, and Apaches—had mostly died of smallpox.

Jimmy liked it in New Mexico, living among some hippie

communes, until war broke out with some local badass Spanish, who began shooting at them and killing a few. The Sikhs then bought a machine gun and fired back at the native Mexican Spanish-Indian badasses. Cindy had not been to war and was uneasy, so she left for Tamworth, New Hampshire, to be with her mother. I went with Jimmy, whom I had originally met at Joe Jones's ski shop in North Conway, where he was a salesman. We hitchhiked to Pilar to play cards because we had no money at all, and Jimmy thought he could win a few dollars if our hosts got very drunk late into the night. Jimmy won forty dollars, and we were camping out with a guest host when our gracious hosts began taking potshots at us at six o'clock in the morning. *Bang, bang, bang.*

"That means we are supposed to leave!" said Jimmy with a wide smile, adding, "No time for coffee here this morning. We'll hitch to Taos and buy some on the plaza. We have some money, and we'll get some huevos rancheros with flour tortillas and chili verde."

Jimmy told me he had once been camping in the mountains here with Charles Manson, who had a gang. Some young little hippies overdosed, possibly on heroin or cocaine. Rather than call the police, the Manson gang threw the dead bodies on the bonfire. That took care of that. Then the Mansons moved to Nevada and California to eventually kill a bunch of movie stars, including Sharon Tate at her pool in Beverly Hills. What was left out of that story was that Richard Nixon had authorized with covert money the manufacture of Jacob's Ladder, a type of LSD for the American military to use in battle. Soldiers became psychotic and enjoyed killing with no remorse whatsoever. There were laboratories funded by our own government all over the United States of America, giving this stuff away at discount prices to any young or old hippy wanting to be a guinea pig for experimentation.

Jimmy then brought his Ecuadorian girlfriend to Silverton, Colorado, where I had bought a mining claim and had been host to a handful of college graduate hippies from Ohio who had now run off to new adventures. Shawn was her name because she had at least one gringo parent. She made chipettes, which were between pancakes and tortillas but were very delicious. Jimmy made his coffee while I attended the fire or the stove. We had a view of twin peaks over thirteen thousand feet. We were in my cabins that were beyond rustic, on a mining claim eleven miles from town. It was all uphill to this cabin site at 11,940 feet on the side of Bonita Peak.

I am not sure why we ever left, but Shawn probably wanted to take a bath in town. We ran for water up there to nearby streams but had no running water to speak of.

Jimmy went to Washington, DC, to teach many others the great lessons he had learned because I was not the best of students. He died there in 2010 among other Vietnam War veterans and a whole flock of very devoted friends, I am sure.

INCA AND SON
OF HUASCAR

From my cave beneath the mountain lake,
I did swim with a reed in my mouth
To breathe the thin Andean air.
I did sneak up upon my enemies unaware,
Stealthily like the *Serpiente,*
With condor talons
And eyes of the puma—
Even the stealth of Zorro.
Yes, the speed of the morning rays of the awakening sun
To the Valley of Cusco
Became mine and my inheritance.
I brought in sand and loam
To improve it for Pachamama,
My mother the Earth.
The women and children
Deserve my protection;
I did even better,
Adding Huaylas's whole mountain valleys.
I will be great.
I will rise up like Huascaran.
I will create my dominion over all the earth,
Now that the true God has revealed Himself to me
In the glorious scripture of *Santa Biblia* (the Bible),

Because You alone, Sr. Soledad, are my Creator.
I had been vanquished and defeated at the height of my empire
By those proclaiming Your ransom.
You have laid down Your perfect life
For the sake of my liberty and freedom
From evil and ignorance.
What more could I possibly ask from Thee?
I am humbled before Your presence;
I am lowly; like a snail or a worm,
I crawl upon the earth,
Like Nebucanezzar eating the grass and mooing.
What can I do to raise my fallen comrades from death
That You have not already done?
I am no God;
I am only a man,
A fleeting shadow upon the earth.
Without You, I am nothing at all,
Less than a speck of sand
At the bottom of the ocean.

So speak to me, because
You are all-powerful and I am weak,
Dying little by little
From the moment of my birth.
Life is now fading away:
I am but a skeleton of
My former youthful, vain radiance,
Which I have just left behind
For this world of shadows
In a sunless sea.
Strike every one of us down that offend Thee!
We imagined success was by our own hands,
But all hands are on deck, Lord—
All hands are Thine.
You alone give life.
All the earth and skies are the work

Of Your hands alone,
Because You are the power.
We are but rays of dust,
The tiniest electrons sent by the sun,
Whereas You are all light itself and love.

So shine Your lamp upon us
That we might behold truth:
There is none but Thee.
We are but shadows cast from Thy brightness,
Our lives mere specks of sand on the Atacama Desert
In the hourglass of eternity.
O raise me up, make me great again,
Your Son everlasting!
I was but a snail and a worm crawling lowly,
But I prayed for salvation,
Metamorphosed, and became a butterfly
That had been a worm in wormwood.
I took flight into Your shining brilliance
Because You are above all the stars in heaven.
None can compare: You know everything,
So You alone can change everything.
So please change me!
Make me Your Son
That all men shall wonder
At Thine miracles and behold Thine countenance,
And likewise be disciples of Thee.
Amen.

MAN WITH CAMEL, PART 8

A MAN IS CROSSING THE DESERT ON HIS CAMEL. THEY ARRIVE AT A cliff in front of them, a sheer rock wall straight up. The camel lies down in the sand. The man scratches his head, which is quite sweaty from the long trip in the hot sun.

Now what do I do? he meditates. He keeps meditating and finally falls asleep under a lone tree. He dreams.

He is in Kansas at a Christian church, where everyone is singing. They are waiting, patient, while praying fervently for Jesus to return to the Earth.

It is a very long song, or two or three, lasting three hours without a break. He is growing thirsty while listening to them and finally fakes a trip to the bathroom so he can drink some water and give his ears a break. Jesus won't be coming back today or tonight or tomorrow. He is fairly sure that God himself is quite content to be in heaven, a far better place requiring no electricity because the lights are on up there twenty-four seven.

These charismatic devotees are exhausting themselves with this false hope that Jesus is going to return next week or next month if they make enough Christian folk music. For one thing, the times have changed, and there are no Roman soldiers. For another thing, people are better educated and better informed than Lazarus.

There are now hospitals to raise the dead with far less effort, plus antibiotics.

It's all very well and good to worship God, but you need a job and a place to live. Therefore, you need some time to carry on with these other endeavors. The ultimate prize from all this worship and praise is to return home to the House of Israel, your true home, where you pay the rent or taxes.

So if he ever gets in a word with these sincere Christian cultists, what will it be? Is the pastor trying to procreate for Christ and replicate more pastors in his image, or something like that? There has to be a catch somewhere. This is all too good to be true.

"God is love, and love no one but God himself!" says a passerby on his way to the bathroom to drink water possibly, or reinsert his earplugs. The pastor of this church has had some deep revelation from God that the end-time will be very, very soon, so everyone is to keep praying twenty-four seven.

That is what they are doing: praising God while strumming the guitar, beating the drums, and playing the piano.

"We can move mountains!" exclaims the preacher, which reminds the man of something.

"Yes, move this mountain in front of me!" mumbles the man, waking up to find himself staring at the cliff in front of him. There are two ways to circumvent this cliff: over to the left, where rise cold, snowy mountains, or over to the right, where there are more cold, snowy, high mountains. Should he flip a coin? No, that is sacrilegious. He pulls a cell phone out of his pocket and calls 911. How brilliant an idea this is!

There is no tower in the area, so there is no connection, unless maybe the space station flies overhead tonight. It is larger than Venus and Saturn combined. He has to remember why he made this long trip across several continents. Perhaps it was to get better acquainted with his camel? Surely there is ample time for that now, because he has been on the road so many days that he has lost count.

There were some very cute young ladies in that church, but so much constant prayer has probably depleted them of their vitamins. The pastor may even have depleted them of their virginity for the sake of increasing members of the church. The man builds a fire at the base of the cliff to see which way the smoke goes—left or right? He doesn't want to travel against the wind in any desert. He's done that before.

The smoke goes straight up into the sky.

"How weird!" reflects the man.

While watching the smoke rise, he sees some writings on the rock cliff, six feet above the ground. Someone else has been here.

"If you made it this far, you are one lucky SOB."

Luckily, the man brought his own deck of cards, and he starts playing solitaire. He learned this game from his wife, who taught him in the second year of their marriage. She was feeling the two-year itch and wanted to teach him something useful for his future.

All of his life had been like a game of solitaire. No one had ever wanted to go where he wanted to go. So much for relationships, because in compromise both parties feel cheated. Now he felt quite sleepy. The sun had just set, and it was a good time to sleep because there was now little else to do. He slept and again began to dream ...

He is crossing the desert, and by great good fortune he has a camel. There are very high, insurmountable mountains on the horizon. The wind picks up into a full gale. A sandstorm is approaching from the west. It will be a good time to hide behind some rocks. He hunkers down as grains of sand fly by at seventy miles per hour. He thinks about his loneliness and realizes he must be happy because there was no compromise in getting here, where no other being would want to be. It is his place in time and his place on earth. This must be home. He digs with his shovel into the earth. The kitchen will be on this side of the house, facing easterly.

The Word of God is that He is good and will dwell in the House of Israel forever. Then let this be God's house that the travelers who pass by have some shelter from the storm. The Christians will take the road to the left; the Hebrews will go right. The Buddhists and Sikhs may want to scale the cliff straight ahead in the distance. The Hindus and Muslims ... I do not yet know their travel plans. Should they come in peace, they will be welcome; should they come otherwise, there is a bear or else a puma in the backyard to take care of their aggressions ...

WE WILL BECOME GOOD SOLDIERS IN THE ARMY OF ONE (WE LIKEWISE SHALL JOIN THEM SOON)

Those who carried the dead and dying

On 9/11, in New York, 2001,

Have joined the list of casualties of that terrorist attack

Eighteen years ago when Manhattan burned,

Asbestos burned, plastic burned, bodies burned, arms and legs …

When people held hands and jumped from high buildings,

When hearts ached with a hurt that would never heal completely.

They are heroes now too, not because they died on 9/11.

Heroes now because they lived through that horror.

They kept their jobs—they breathed that filthy air of death and destruction.

Heroes now because they were you and me, whose hearts likewise were broken watching their suffering then on television.

Heroes now because they sent their kids through college,

Working overtime, riding subways and buses,

Driving in Long Island traffic over Brooklyn Bridge and Triboro Bridge,

Under Lincoln Tunnel, over Washington Bridge—

I want you to know my heart still bleeds for them.

All of us who grew up in Greater New York and Boston and Philadelphia and America,

We remember that day when so many had fallen from the sky and from airplanes with no parachutes.

Now they are still falling by the wayside, but there is some hope,

There is some hope that we cherish deep in our hearts for brave people like them.

The brave people who lived through 9/11 and every terror attack all over the planet,

We salute them for their bravery, we salute them for living courageously

With broken hearts like our own, yet we now live on a few more months and years.

We remember them; they had faces and voices and dreams.

They were never alone, nor are we, because we love each other.

We love them for their bravery and stamina, which inspires us still.

They have now gone to live with the angels in a better world,

Where truth and justice reign supreme,

Where God now wipes away their every tear.

They can see God now because they knew God then deep in their hearts.

They know still that we are all one.

Yes, we are, and we are brave, and we are proud,

Proud of our God who unites us to all be brothers and sisters in this battlefield of life.

There are no winners but those who trust in God; in God we all trust,

That we likewise shall join them too in heaven and sing.

We shall sing Hallelujah, we shall praise our God,

Who has brought us through all this suffering and into grace and perfection.

We who believe and trust our Lord shall deliver,

We will all be good soldiers in the army of one.

MRS. STONE AND THE
MOUNTAIN SHAPED
LIKE A VOLCANO

THERE WAS A GUY, JOHN ROTH, WHO CAME TO SILVERTON AND BOUGHT the Grand Imperial Hotel, a relic of the turn of the century— not this one but the last, 1900.

It was in a sad state of affairs, but John Roth had either money or credit, his Anglo-Saxon ancestors going back to the American Revolution and George Washington. He had both. Therefore it was restored. I may even have worked there a day or two as a laborer; with none of the necessary skills, I was let go, fired. It was hard not to come back to the place, its bar was out of the late eighteen hundreds in those days, when gold and silver were discovered in great abundance in Colorado, an inhospitable state with winter nighttime temperatures in the mountains of about thirty below zero in January. The erected wooden shacks housing the miners had no insulation in the walls nor foundations, but coal was in abundance, finally brought in by the narrow gauge railroad from Durango. Although Red Mountain had a railroad from Ouray and the north, where Somerset had coal, so did Hesperus to the west of Durango, the home terminal of the Silverton Galloping Goose, which defied avalanches and hailstorms to ferry its passengers and cargo to Silverton.

About ninety years later, a hairdresser from New York City arrived with her slightly younger husband, who served more as her valet. She recently had a dream in New York of acquiring vast wealth, and she went to her good friend the fortune teller, who confirmed her intuitions that in a high mountain in Colorado out west, shaped like a volcano, near Silverton, she would discover a vein of gold leading straight down into Middle Earth itself—immeasurable wealth like the Orient itself, like all the Incas and Pizarro combined. She sold her salon and managed to borrow money from investor-speculators, and she pulled her husband by the ear across the Great Plains to look at the spectacular Rocky Mountains and see a mountain shaped like a volcano near Silverton. There it was. She spotted it and went to the local real estate broker, feigning to buy a large house on main street, which she did. Then she added that she didn't know what to do with the rest of her very large sum of money.

"Well, you might speculate in patented mining claims and wait for the price of gold to come back up!" offered the realtor, who thought of her as some Eastern fool. Everyone knew FDR took America off the gold standard, ever since mining had gone to hell. Now there was this woman who seemingly wanted to go to hell with it?

"Yes, that's such a pretty mountain, and my husband can build a summer home up there from all those large spruce trees. Are they really over two hundred years old?" She bought every available mining claim on that thirteen-thousand-foot peak, both patented and unpatented. The realtor was beginning to suspect something, but what did he care as his commissions were even larger on mining claims?

My Ohio friends, who were students recently at Ohio State but had hitchhiked into town to drink beer at the Grand Imperial Hotel, lived at my cabins as guests for several months with no employment, or almost none at all. They went to town for beer and met some very exquisite lady with a valet husband she pulled around by his ascot. This lady and her husband were wearing cowboy hats of the best quality but were obviously New Yorkers, with no horses in sight anywhere. There was a very large four-wheel-drive Land Cruiser outside. The lady promptly hired them both, plus a Caterpillar driver who would bulldoze her a road to that summit of her golden mountain.

"Oh, isn't it beautiful!" she exclaimed, looking at the majestic mountain but more at the gold inside of it. Off they all drove, and the bulldozer made it all the way up there, pulling two sledges, one a luxury trailer, the finest money could buy, and the other exactly the opposite, a quarters for the help with a wood stove but not so well made. It suffered some damage on the long trip up there, so there were several cracks in the walls that needed to be stuffed with rags. Also, its roof leaked. The weather still wasn't too bad at the end of October, but then a howling wind came, which was the advent of winter, and it soon snowed, snowed, and kept snowing while the wind did not abate at all.

Mrs. Stone, dressed in her minks, barked orders for her motley crew of two, my friends Nick and Gus. "Dig, dig, dig straight down. Use those picks. Here, my husband will bring the dynamite." *Bang! Bang!* They were on their way to China or hell, whichever might appear first.

Meanwhile, at the bottom of the mountain, the bulldozer slid in all that snow, flipping over and killing its driver. They were now cut off on top of that peak with enough supplies for the Chinese Army, if they should discover it.

Of course, it turned out there was no gold, and my friends were waiting to get their final paycheck when Mrs. Stone slipped out of town at 3:00 a.m., never to be seen again, with creditors looking for her from coast to coast. Rumor had it she made it to San Francisco to open a brothel or something. All these are just rumors, because this entire story was made up by Nick and Gus for me to believe. However, the bulldozer driver did die. Life is hard in the Rockies, and Silverton was no exception.

Gus went off to Pilar, New Mexico, with Nick and Jimmy, and they cultivated marijuana. But not Jimmy, who left for New Hampshire and Washington, DC.

They were about to reap a very large harvest when Gus saw Mount Zion and God, who told him to throw his portion of the marijuana in the Rio Grande River across the street. Nick ran off with his share to sell it to Mrs. Stone or whoever might buy it, and he wasn't heard from because he probably soon got free room and board up the river somewhere. Gus, after seeing Jesus and the angels, returned to Toledo to be a good Catholic, marry, raise a family, and be saintly. It was rumored Mrs. Stone died shortly thereafter, so her creditors got burned in hell, as they say.

SHUNNED BY BEATTIE
IN ASPEN, THEN
INVITED TO IPSRA

N 1966, I HAD WON THE MT. SNOW CUP, THE STOWE CUP, AND THE Eastern Championships (both slalom and giant slalom, although I was runner-up in the wildcat downhill to Mike Raymaley). I won the Baxter Cup and then proceeded to be second place in the North Americans GS, and so won Athlete of the Month for New Hampshire and dinner with the governor, Meldrim Thompson.

With some added political pressure from Roger Peabody of USEASA (begrudged by Beattie), I was placed on the US ski team traveling to Europe in 1967, where I placed ninth in the Bormio downhill behind Paul Marysko, a Czechoslovakian (begrudged by Gordi Eaton, US Men's alpine ski coach). Rebel Ryan finished second. We were held up by a snowstorm and arrived a day late for Kitzbuhel, Austria, Hahnenkahm, and missed the first day of downhill training. Trying to make up for lost time, I skied too aggressively in the Steilhang fallaway turn and cartwheeled into the woods and into a tree well, where I was greeted by the Canadian National Ski team members Yogi Rod Hebron and Peter Duncan.

Gordi Eaton decided that I should be locked in my hotel room overnight while he and the rest of the team enjoyed beer in the tavern (possibly because I was nineteen years old). Unfortunately, the room had no bathroom and no running water. I was dehydrated but woken up by Gordi and freed at seven next morning. I waited in the dining room for some breakfast. The waiter smiled at me and looked very familiar; he was a laughing, tall blond man, mostly bald. Had I seen him before? On the television mounted on the wall, I watched Jean Claude Killy win the ski race before I even left the hotel to board the tram car. My number given to me by Beattie in the draw was 125 out of 126 racers. I was to run second from last. Oh, well. Almost late for my start and still dehydrated, I looked between my ski boots down at the course and pushed off at "Aus," which meant *go*.

I set the hill record for my missed pre-jump before the first turn, inspiring the Austrian press to write that Americans were not coached how to pre-jump. My skis skidded out in the Steilhung turn, and I finished a dismal fifty-seventh, the fifth American.

Gordi Eaton had some encouraging words. "You were eleventh fastest on the lower half of the course. What did you do in the Steilhang?"

Rebel Ryan planned our late-night escape in Bormio, where we planned to steal some Italian flags as souvenirs, but these were discovered in our luggage. I was sent home a week early from the Munich airport, escorted there by Gordi Eaton, who told me to stop staring at the German bombshell women.

In 1968, I broke my collarbone while running downhill on Cannon Mountain, my home hill. I missed most of that season.

In 1969, I won the Steamboat, Colorado, slalom, but before my run in the downhill, Bill Marolt and his buddies put a kicker lip on the first jump before I was to run, and my number was dead last. My friends forewarned me, so I snowplowed beforehand and still almost fell, finishing dead last in the downhill but still tasking second in the combined. It crossed my mind that they thought I was Jewish.

I won the Colorado Cup slalom at Winter Park and, despite running twenty-ninth in the Roche Cup, Aspen, finished second in that slalom. The Europeans were coming to Aspen for a World Cup, and Beattie sent out the race invitations to deserving Americans. I was not included.

I went to see Bob Beattie in his office to ask him why I was excluded. He laughed. I lunged forward with a right hook to hit him but was restrained from behind by his personal bodyguard, Greg Lewis.

I stood up in the final slalom at Jackson Hole to win the overall High Country Trophy, which was the overall championship of the Rockies and Sierras. Ann Black won the women's version. I returned to New Hampshire, where, because sixty feet of snow had fallen on Mt. Washington, it was decided to hold that famous race last held in 1939: the American Inferno, from the summit of Mt. Washington over the lip of the headwall at Tuckerman's Ravine. The Little Headwall had collapsed into the raging brook below the ravine, opening an insurmountable crevasse, so the ski race finish line would have to be the bottom of the Ravine. Lucky for me, because my stamina from a poor lifestyle would probably have been insufficient for the two-mile ski trail all the way to Pinkham Notch. A snowcat ferried the racers to Howard Johnson's the nickname of the Appalachian Mountain hut at the four-thousand-foot elevation halfway up the mountain, where I tarried too long and was behind the other racers climbing the two thousand vertical feet to the summit. A very tight turn had been set in the course by John Clough, my former rival, who told the Palmer brothers, my current rivals, "This is where Duncan Cullman will fall, ha ha." I did, but the mountain was so steep behind me, it pushed me back up over my skis, and I completed that turn, losing less than a second. I still won the race. Tyler Palmer was not himself that day and took second place at only eighteen years of age. David Reed from Seattle and Dartmouth took third. Terry Palmer fell above the lip and had only one ski left on his feet, but he used it to redirect his dangerous direction toward the famous crevasses on the lip that had killed so many. Gerry Knapp had not been invited to the race, perhaps for the same reasons I had not been invited by Beattie to the Aspen World Cup. Jean Claude Killy and Karl Schranz were at the ski show in New York but declined their invitations because the USSA would not sanction the race for the Federation International du Ski (FIS), so their insurance would not cover them. Plus, they probably wanted money to compete. Hank Kashiwa was in the US Army at Ft. Carson, tending amputees, and was not notified in time, so he could not attend. Bobby Cochran was only seventeen years old and finished eighth. Jeff Bruce was fifteen years old and finished last but not least. Peter Carter, Bill McCollom, and Tom Acker were fourth, fifth, and sixth, respectively.

A year later, an ex SS storm trooper for Nazi Germany, Willi Schaeffler, now the new American national ski coach, expelled me from all major US Ski competitions, and he was backed up by Frederick Lounsberry, now president of USEASA. They had reasons to believe I was a hippie and homeless.

I had nowhere to go but sent my apologies to Bob Beattie to please let me join his new franchise, International Professional Ski Racers Association. I was already famous, and he relented.

THE PRISONERS

ONE SUMMER WHEN I WAS BEGINNING A MIDLIFE CRISIS AND SUFFERING from undiagnosed thyroid failure, the Sugar Hill chief of police, who was actually also the chief of the Lisbon, New Hampshire, Police Department, pulled me over in my old fart's car, an older Buick.

"Mr. Kuhlman," he addressed me, "your license has been revoked!"

Of course I had been hoping that by some miracle it hadn't been revoked.

There was a court date and a heavy fine of three hundred dollars. The judge said, "Mr. Cullman, if you are caught driving with a suspended license again, you will serve up to one year in prison."

I was determined not to let that happen, and I rode my bicycle uphill against the wind and traffic over a mile each way daily to the Coffee Pot Diner. It was the highlight and zenith of my every waking day. Of course, there were indeed some better days when I was picked up by our commissioner of senior softball, Clifton Crosby, to play in an afternoon softball league, which was even more fun than drinking coffee. Thus passed my entire summer. My motel room was almost like a prison, except for the television and its History Channel featuring Adolf Hitler welcoming Hans Rudel, Stuka pilot, into the underground bunker in Berlin to receive the Golden Oak Leaves, the highest Nazi medal, at 3:00 a.m. Eastern my time, sixty years after the event had actually taken place.

Now we have this pandemic and are confined to our homes except for groceries and gas in 2020.

I was fifteen years old in 1963 when I received a letter from Lucy in Little Compton, Rhode Island: "Dear Duncan, come and visit me in Rhode Island."

I bought a train ticket with some money I had probably stolen from my drunken father's wallet. He had plenty. Of course, when I got to Rhode Island, it was a bit more difficult, but Lucy's older sister came with a car to pick me up."

Lucy was fifteen too, and she said, "Come with me to the beach."

I did, and quite soon we were rolling in the sand and then kissing. Then she was grabbing me to penetrate her, but I had never, and it was all sandy, and seagulls were flying overhead and screeching. We were not entirely successful, but nothing quite like this had ever happened to me before; she evidently was the more experienced. Actually, I knew about her from the Samson's Ski Chalet in Mad River Glen, Vermont, and heard that she had gone all the way with a seventeen-year-old in the absentee parent's bedroom.

Fifteen years later, Ed Rodgers, the director of New England Peugeot Pro Ski Tour, told me that Lucy was indeed living near his bar in Farmington.

I knocked on the door. Lucy opened it and finally recognized me.

"Come on in, but you can't stay here because I have a jealous boyfriend who is a state trooper. If he knows you stayed here, he will beat you up or arrest you!"

She relented and let me sleep over because I had nowhere to go and little money. We ski racers didn't make much. I suppose Ed Rogers knew our ski parents were all rich.

The next day, I competed in the final ski race of the year at Sugarloaf but fell on my second run and was eliminated. Nonetheless, everyone was in an end-of-season party mood. The ski area bars were full with us beer drinkers and cocktail waitresses in leotards and lipstick. I did an exhibition ski jump that was almost suicidal as I flew thirty feet high off the snow and then crash-landed, ejecting from my bindings and cutting my forehead and nose on the abrasive, icy spring snow. I was covered in blood and a few bandages. I entered a bar and saw Frank Rogers, Ed's brother. He told me to settle down and behave. I told him a thing or two about us "pro" ski racers being underpaid. His friend told me to shut up, or he would handcuff me. I had heard enough with too much adrenaline circulating in my blood still, so I decided to take a swing.

Next thing I knew, I was being chased by Frank's friend and his followers out of the bar and into the snow.

"Hold him down till I get the cuffs in my truck," Frank's friend commanded.

They were pummeling me and fractured my skull, but I reached out and grabbed a nearby slalom pole. I swung it to drive them off of me. I ran away barefoot in the snow, going up the mountain. They had stolen my ski boots off my feet. It was now getting dark, and they were chasing me on snowmobiles, but I found a hole and covered myself with snow. They did not see me and raced off.

I entered a lift shack that had an electric heater and string, plus some Styrofoam insulation and plastic bags. I made mukluks out of those materials, so now I had warm feet. I escaped all evening until just past midnight, when I decided to hitch a ride. It was Mike Collins, Ed Rogers's assistant, who said, "Get in. Are you all right? Every cop in the state is looking for you. Take my truck and drive somewhere. I'll tell them you must have stolen it. Here are the keys. Get out of this state."

He left me there in his pickup and ran off somewhere so as not to be my accomplice. Unfortunately, I had no money, and the fuel tank was near empty.

What was worse was that my skull was fractured, and I had serious brain issues, a throbbing headache, and hypothermia. Therefore I turned myself in from a phone booth at 7:00 a.m.

The judge banged his wooden mallet and said, "Six months," which seemed like an overly stern sentence to me because I had been in bar brawls out west and only once had done two days.

It was determined there were lice in our county jail, and the exterminators showed up with masks and pesticide, spraying everything and everyone. We had no masks, so everyone else was let outside, but not me. My skull was slowly healing even though I was denied medical attention.

After nine weeks, my father's CIA contact, Hans Rudel, showed up and bribed the jailer to let me out of the prison to run around in the yard for exercise. Rudel is long gone now. I would never see him again because he died within four years, back in Germany.

Outside the jail, I could hear some pretty young ladies talking across the street. One gave the other her own name and address. I wrote a letter from inside the jail. To the surprise of the guards, some young ladies from across the street baked some cookies for the prisoners. My extra privileges were suspended, and I was put in solitary, but then a burglar was put in there with me.

"Watch this," I told him, and I held the water switch on. Soon we were standing in two feet of water. It was leaking through the floor and onto the secretaries below us. The chief of police didn't really care because he wanted a new jail to be built.

My father finally came to my rescue, hired a lawyer, and appealed my case.

It turned out in the investigation that Frank Rodger's friend at the bar was Lucy's state cop boyfriend. She had warned me, "He'll beat you up or arrest you!"

My sentence was commuted to time served, about five months. However, it was a plea deal, and my conviction was not overturned.

Now that the coronavirus is here, in this pandemic I feel badly for those who have never lost their freedom, have never served, or have never done time in a prep school. Some of us went to Holderness, which was one such in New Hampshire. At the twenty-fifth class reunion, I took notice that no one in my class attended. Our headmaster hated skiers and picked on us like we were all Peck's bad boy. He was a real humdinger.

This coronavirus prison at home is really not so bad after all. We have television and movies, plus we can write down our stories for future movies. People are dying everywhere, especially in the big cities. Those who never lost their freedom have no discipline at all, perhaps, not that the rest of us live in a perfect heaven. We know this is closer to hell and know what to expect next.

NOW THAT WAR
IS HERE

Now that war is here and has found us,

We declare ourselves to be the peacemakers against this virus.

For we are soldiers, Christian soldiers as well.

We have our righteous duties to be vigilant and perform.

This new pandemic virus sent from God,

Our St. Adversity to refine us like gold and make our hearts pure,

So that we graduate in grace and enter the kingdom of heaven to be like our God,

Immortal and indestructible though our earthly bodies are not.

We shall shed them in time for new bodies to be like angels on high,

To be like cherubs and seraphim arriving at our new posts.

Stand vigilant in this new fight and be courageous.

It is all the creation of our Lord God, the king of heavenly hosts.

The long-awaited hour of Armageddon is upon us,

So chose which side you shall continue to fight for.

It is never too late to repent and join the winning side.

Our Lord God shall prevail once again as always.

We must put behind us our former sinful ways, shedding them forever,

To reaffirm what is pure in our hearts:

That we belong to our Lord God and exist only to fulfill His divine purpose.

The grand plan was created before time even existed.

The armies are drawing up each one on its cherished soil.

Yet one side shall not prevail but shall be extinguished forever.

So stand with the God who created you,

And if you are a demon, then so be it a final ending for you at last.

One shall reap what one has sowed.

The peace of God be with you, and mercy that you will not suffer.

There will be crying and gnashing of teeth.

Be no longer wicked or covetous for pleasures of this earth, for they are short lived.

Therefore, take your stand for your God and be his, be his soldier of truth and righteousness.

God himself shall be your breastplate and armor.

Whether or not you live or die upon this earth, there shall be created for you a place in heaven eternal.

That is all you need to know, because you have faith who are most faithful.

Let yourself not be cast out into the desert with the jackals to perish in loneliness.

Your brothers and sisters, all children of God await you.

Come to them all to this place, Zion, where they await you and prepare a feast.

You are to be an honored guest at this banquet to be held in your honor,

Now that you have come home to the family of God.

Your Father still loves you and has forgiven you. Repent!

MAN, CAMEL, AND
GOD (PART 6)

AMAN OF **G**OD RIDES HIS CAMEL IN THE DESERT.
It begins to snow. This is not an everyday occurrence. This is not an ordinary man but one whose life was changed miraculously by the hand of God.

Of course he had been raised in his father's house. That was very long ago and just a memory. There had been servants who cared for his upbringing. His father was there for breakfast very early and home very late because he worked long hours at his business. Our man had been raised by a handful of servants and the family dogs, which were well fed and amiable as well. There was of course the cook, who prepared the food, and she sometimes took him to market. There was her husband, the roofer, who sometimes cut the grass or cleaned the yard. There was the launderer, who washed all the dirty clothes and changed the bedsheets. There was the baker, who rolled the dough and made the bread. There was the plumber, who fixed the clogged toilets, and his friend the electrician, who added wires and changed the light bulbs. There was the pet sitter, who fed the dogs, and the realtor, who had sold the house but wanted to relist it and sell it again. There was the policeman, who followed his father home and reprimanded him, "Do not drink and drive again, or I'll have to arrest you and take your license!" There were so many fond memories of such a grand house, with so many workers to keep it safe and secure.

Now, the boy grew into a man with a love of all animals because the dogs were well fed and amiable. The camel was well fed in a large desert but hadn't eaten since early morning. The sun went down, and the stars finally came out. It stopped snowing, and the wind picked up.

"Where will I meet the woman with a camel?" he wondered. Perhaps it was time to settle down, buy a house, and raise a family with well-fed, amiable dogs and cats—even a parakeet!

The moon rose up over a hill and illuminated the vast wasteland. Had God forgotten this place? Had God forgotten to tell the clouds to water the grass and plants here? Where had God gone off to in such haste to only return briefly in a rare snow flurry? God was indeed just like his own father, off and running to some far location, busy, busy, busy somewhere.

It was time to remember his mother. She was sick, perhaps from smoking so many cigarettes or drinking endless pots of coffee. She worried and did her Rosary but was a bundle of nerves, so she took sleeping pills. The doctor came to the house and prescribed even more pills for her to take after each exam. Finally she took so many pills that she did not wake up one morning. There was a funeral for her, and all the house servants came. Father kissed the coffin, which was lowered into the ground. If only she had some work to do herself, maybe she would have lived longer and not taken so many pills. Maybe she should have taken a job in town as a sales clerk in a boutique. Maybe she had her hands full being a mother?

The camel stopped to eat a tumbleweed or two. The early morning light filled the eastern horizon. The man needed to sleep himself. The camel was dozing. It had been a long journey in this foreboding world, which lacked the comfort of a secure home full of so many gracious servants. The house was more than just a house; it was a home filled with people all working. His mother had been a mother, which was a job of sorts, yes. No one was lazy there. No one was a bum, or the house would have fallen down in disrepair.

That is what the father does: he goes to work in order to have a home to live in and sleep at night. He sleeps very well because he is of good conscience from working so hard to pay all those bills and many servants.

Happy and secure is the home of the Lord, the house of Israel that believes in the Lord our living God, who likewise does not slumber.

THADDEUS THORNE

THADDEUS THORNE ENLISTED IN THE TENTH MOUNTAIN DIVISION, WINTER warfare specialists of the US Army. He was found to be an outstandingly bright young soldier, so he was sent to officer training school for a few months. When he returned to Camp Hale, Colorado, he learned his unit had been shipped out to Italy without him, but he would be needed to fight the Japanese in the jungles of the Pacific Arena.

We make plans to do this and that, when suddenly war breaks out and our lives are changed forever. We imagine there will be some war with Rocket Man, the North Korean dictator, when suddenly we find ourselves at war with a virus.

The world turns, and we turn this way and that with it.

The challenge of history is, Will you be able to keep up with the fast pace of our changing world, or will you be left behind? I was left behind by my first wife, who filed for divorce out of the clear blue sky. Suddenly, she and my children were gone out of my life and swept under my father's financial empire to become his personal allies against me.

So what will become of us now that evil is having its day again with death and destruction? Here, we have a virus possibly invented by man under God's direction, because all creation is just that. Perhaps God wants us all to unite and stop our partisan bickering? We were long overdue for a correction. So was the stock market as well, evidently.

There is some outdated drug used to fight malaria ineffectively, and perhaps that somehow works well against COVID-19, but for how long? Eventually the virus will mutate once again into a new strain resistant to any malaria drug. Social distancing will become the new norm, and shaking hands will be a forgotten ritual of the past.

God is evidently not terribly pleased by our human behavior and wishes to mold us in grace and charity for all, with new human suffering displayed twenty-four seven on every television channel in HD and 5.1 surround sound.

There is growing anxiety worldwide. This is like a bad dream that reoccurs daily and on every nightly news show. Thus, we who are writers recording these grave events are now war correspondents on the front lines of this pandemic that threatens our very existence. We knew this great reduction of world population was inevitable, but we hoped maybe it would be the next generation, not our own, to face it. We are consistently wrong.

The new and unforeseen is a daily occurrence, and we hold no crystal globe in which we can foretell the future. All the Antarctic ice is melting. The sea is rising. Our cities are flooding and then burning.

Chaos is still in our world, reigning almost supreme. Can it be we have forgotten God in our gluttonous consumerism? So where is the road home for us to peace and tranquility? Too boring, you say? Then be entertained by this plague as it strikes your family because you are self-destructive. So be it.

Thaddeus Thorne likewise had no idea where he was going as he next hit the beach at Guadalcanal. Now we are hitting that beach with him. Now we are in Saipan and Bataan, Philippines and Okinawa. This is war!

MAN ON A CAMEL

GOD WILL TELL ME WHAT TO WRITE ABOUT THIS MAN I AM TO BE.
I trust that God knows every story and will tell me what to
write.

A man was crossing the desert on a camel. He came to an oasis
that had a well. He was very thirsty, and he began to drink and fill his
canteen.

"This is private property, and this water you drink will have to
be paid for," announced the approaching local sheik. The man had no
money and was arrested and thrown into debtor's prison. Then he was
taken before the local judge.

"I am saddened that you have no money to pay," said the judge,
adding, "Now you will be sold into slavery in order to pay off your
debt!"

So the man was sold to a caravan of gypsies passing through the
land. They had many animals to care for because they were a traveling
circus. There were tigers, monkeys, elephants, kangaroos, and birds in
cages. The many animals depended on this man for their welfare.

God looked down from heaven and saw this man struggling in his
daily labors. He was no longer a selfish man acting in his own interest
but instead caring for many other living creatures.

He did not free the man from his servitude because he was now
a better man with a big family, even if it was an animal family. It was
still that: a family.

You thought you were going somewhere in your life, traveling on a
highway, when God intervened and took you to a new place. Now you

have a family to feed, and your former selfish life has passed away. You are going to grow up and assume your new responsibilities. This will lead you into the happiness and bliss you were missing in your former selfish life. It is as though you have taken on a whole new life and been born again. You have been rescued from your selfish, self-destructive life and been resurrected into a new, angelic life eternal. Love itself is eternal, love is God. Now, be good! If you want to stay out of jail, get a job because everyone must serve someone—or go nuts like our president.

PART Z FROM PAGE 43—SKIING IN PERU (BEGINNING WITH JOHN STIRLING)

LUIS WILL ACCOMPANY HER TO THE BUS STATION BECAUSE SHE HAS BEEN there six weeks, studying and teaching kindergarten in the school of orphans and being a part-time soccer coach.

Downtown Huaraz is a good two-mile walk from my living quarters.

I take a cafe executive, including papaya juice and a meat empanada and cafe au lait, when I run into my tour guide of yesterday, Lauro, who beckons me to his office. For a mere sixteen dollars, I buy an all-day bus ticket, including a guide for an all-day adventure learning the culture and history of Peru.

My childhood friend, a very young man himself then at twenty, just seven years my senior, whom I met skiing in Portillo, Chile, in 1963 fifty-one years ago, is now deceased, but the memory of him lives on.

He would reach his hand out to shake the hand of even the most downtrodden Hell's Angel, or cowboy, or rail-riding hobo. e had big white teeth and a wide smile, and his ancestors surely did come from Stirling Castle in Scotland, dwelling place of nobles and kings.

John grew up in Florida, where his archeologist parents bought land

and sold a portion of it to move back to San Francisco. They bought apartments with WWII government loans, which they rented out.

Then they bought a house in Aspen, Colorado, and acreage down valley in Carbondale on Missouri Heights, which is quite similar to the puma pampas of Peru in some regards because it was remote.

John Stirling and I eventually competed in national ski competitions over several years, with successes mostly in slalom.

He divorced his first gold-digger wife, Nancy, and then met and married Ruthie. They had four daughters.

John would take his family sailing on the high seas, something he must have learned in Florida from his parents, who must have discovered El Dorado, the hidden Spanish gold, to have bought so much real estate.

Some sections of sailing in Asia are a bit dangerous because there are pirates, so Ruthie and the girls stayed home in Carbondale, in the house with the copper roof, while John recruited his more hardy friend Crazy Charlie, and off they sailed to Bali and Madagascar, meeting people in every port, including Haifa in Israel.

John's good handshake and confidence were displayed in his wide, toothy smile behind rather large biceps from wrestling and boxing. You had to smile back. Everyone could tell he was a confident fighter, so everyone would very quickly decide it's better to have him on your side than against you. Under it all, John was against no one, not even against the massive Russian battleship that split his boat in two one dark Pacific night. Luckily, no one was killed.

He was like an eager king ready and fit to meet his troops and prepare them for battle. All men would rally behind him without question for any noble cause. His cause was to be noble and protect the underdog. He was no different than Wallace or De Bruce, like Duncan and his son, Siward Bjornson Armstrong, Scots all.

SKIING NEAR LLAIMA
VOLCANO IN CHILE
WITH RUDEL

N **1960** AT AGE TWELVE, I HAD THE VERY GOOD FORTUNE TO ACCOMPANY my father and his new lady friend, Anne Wing, to Chile in South America. We skied Portillo for over a week and then headed south by DC-3, a two-engine propeller plane that was made popular in World War II, to Temuco, where it never stopped raining. There were many indigenous Chilean natives who were seemingly everywhere. The tall blond man who looked much too familiar hated these dark-skinned people, considering them to be an infernal race of imbeciles.

Where had he come from, and why did he harbor so much resentment? As a child, I could not quite understand such an attitude. Yet in grade school, I had already been taught that the Catholic Church had kept humanity in the Dark Ages until the Renaissance, when science was born.

The ski lodge was very dirty, and smoke filled the entire building whenever the wind blew, which was constantly. I coughed a lot and detested this inferior ski area. It was nothing compared to Portillo, but evidently the blond man had invited us to southern Chile to see his homeland. He looked like someone I had seen before, another one of my father's strange acquaintances in New Canaan, Connecticut. But this was thousands of miles away on a different continent altogether.

When I asked my father about this strange man, he said, "You never saw him. This is a secret meeting for our government. Remember nothing about this man. Forget you ever saw him."

We then traveled to Peru and visited Machu Picchu, which was a jungle snake–infested "hangri La for the Inca Empire.

Maybe at some point Anne Wing left us, because she was no longer needed to make us appear to be a normal tourist family. Just my father and I went to the monastery above Cuzco, where my father knocked loudly on the door. Finally a man answered and summoned the bishop, who informed my father that the person of interest no longer resided there and had gone to Bolivia or maybe Paraguay.

This person of interest was Martin Bormann, Hitler's personal assistant. Had he been hiding in the abbey, dressed up as a friar?

We then flew home because my father was to meet some very important people somewhere. None of this was my business. I had to return to grade school at New Canaan Country Day School, where I would fight Clausen daily over our common girlfriend, Kathy Graham, who doted on all our attention.

THANKSGIVING
IN MAINE

I REMEMBER Thanksgiving in Maine with Sam Hall, the major partner and president of Tenney Mountain Ski Corporation. His grandmother was the Gerber Baby, though I didn't know it at the time. His daughter was Penelope, a Greek goddess of weaving, surely. She had caught my attention while working for her mother in the base lodge cooking hamburgers. Both of them had long blonde locks like Norwegians. Sam, however, was a Pennsylvania Dutch who fancied himself as a German. He drove a Porsche 911 and knew every part of the car, explaining each one of them to me on the long drive to our job in Maine. I was one of his crew and perhaps his most prized one, but his daughter's parts interested me all the more. For one reason or another, auto mechanics didn't interest me all that much. Mechanics were dirty people covered with grease and holding wrenches that were never quite the right one because cars rusted so horribly, their undercarriages were usually unrecognizable.

My own father said I had schizophrenia, a disease and mental disorder. I did have a mental distraction all my teenage years, and that was sex. I wondered whether I would be successful, and when. I didn't care about falling in love and all that mush. Penny was a German too, and she wasn't all that mushy. She wrote me very long letters that I received at Holderness Boarding School. She was my girl, all right. We both knew it.

When would her father acknowledge me as a part of her life? Probably never.

At the Thanksgiving dinner in Maine, I had to promise Sam that I wouldn't utter even one word. Everyone there was a logger, and no one talked. That was the rule in the Maine woods: everyone ate in silence.

There were some things about me I am sure that Sam knew from talking to Mr. French, my foster father. Mr. French had been a high-ranking officer in the US Navy in the Pacific during World War II. His unit had been poised to make an amphibious landing on Japan in which he would have most assuredly been killed when an atomic bomb was dropped on Hiroshima and then on Nagasaki. The war ended without an invasion of Japan itself, and Mr. French was promoted to US intelligence. He knew a lot of stuff he didn't talk about at the dinner table. He would instead say, "You'd better have some more Pepsi!" and pour me another glass. He worked as a shift boss at the Bobbin Mill in Beebe River, New Hampshire, for Draper Corporation. I had met a Willie Draper, who went to Harvard as a freshman but never knew the connection. White America ran everything back then before Martin Luther King Jr. was assassinated. Perhaps they still do.

I had a strange dream back then. I was holding a stick that was supposed to represent my gun. A white man was drilling several of us children. We were dressed in rags. My mother then told me to do everything the man said so that he would choose me to fly with him in his plane, a Russian MIG, but its inscription was German Democratic Republic. The lettering was strange to me, and I spoke Korean, as did my little comrades. We had red flags we waved when the jet fighters took off.

I suppose my dreams were all part of my schizophrenia, which had been far less severe before puberty; then hormones propelled it out of control.

At age four, I was brought to a strange new house in Connecticut from my other home on Cape Cod by the ocean. A strange dog wandered into our new yard. I wanted to name him Rudel, but my new nanny insisted that was not an American name and that Rudolf would suffice. This was a different country, this Connecticut.

There was a tall, balding man with blond hair who kept coming to our house, or my father would meet him at a neutral house in New Canaan, but they rarely met at that man's house in Pound Ridge, New York. I had been there once, though, in that Pound Ridge big red house with a red fence for those springer spaniel hunting dogs.

The blond man's name was Rudel, but nobody said it. His wife was a very stern English lady he had met in England as a prisoner of war. They had two daughters who seemed to be twins and a year or two younger than me. They were very cute, well-dressed young frauleins, highly disciplined and very proper at all times. There was a son somewhere that they all said I was not to meet because the male children were more endangered by fanatical Zionists, the Mossad.

The man, with his one leg amputated and the other leg in a cast, rowed me across the small pond in front of his house. I suppose all that rowing was his exercise. He had a metal plate in his head from the war, if I remember correctly.

Henry Kissinger had recruited him to go back to East Germany as a spy during the Korean War. I was at least fourteen years old and a skier before I heard the name Henry Kissinger. Kennedy, our president, had been shot in Dallas, Texas. It was on every television station and was terrible news. Somehow it didn't bother me that much. I had seen dead bodies, even in South America, when the ski lift broke and ran backward. I was just arriving to get back on it, but all these soldiers were being ejected at the lower bull wheel sharp corner, with the lift going backward at sixty miles an hour. Many yelled as their backs and necks were broken. Terrible carnage. Some ski instructors from Austria skied over to me and covered my eyes so I would not see. Another one yelled, "Get him out of here. He's just a child and doesn't need to see this!"

I'm not sure whether I told that story to Sam Hall. Probably I told him everything. I think he knew my father, who adopted me, was a chief in the CIA.

I was quite thankful to be allowed to move to New Hampshire permanently because my CIA father was much too busy to spend time with me anymore. We had some good years together, especially going on ski vacations to Mount Snow, Bromley, and Mad River Glen. We also went to Llaima, Farrellones, and Portillo, Chile.

My CIA father said that there were a lot of things I should try to forget because it would be in my better interest. I decided Penelope would not be one of them. I had seen her teats, which were enormous; I had fingered her, and that was incredible. Finally, I mounted her in my grandmother's borrowed rental car on the Kancamagus Highway overlook in the White Mountains. I would never forget her even though Sam planned her out of my life. I am very thankful.

I do not speak much at the dinner table because that's what they do up here in the North Woods

HISTORY OF EUROPE

ORIGINALLY, ON THIS EARTH THERE WAS JUST ONE LAND MASS A FEW million years ago. The Earth was not round, or the oceans would have prevailed. The Earth is still not round; it bulges at the equator because its interior is hot liquid.

Due to continental drift, the one large land mass broke into sections we call continents. Europe became a continent, and it was very far north, covered by a big sheet of ice. Possibly the North Pole was closer to Iceland at that time, and that would explain electromagnetic north being different from true north.

The ice began to recede due to global warming. Therefore man, a creature resembling the apes, migrated into Europe from warmer continents like Asia and Africa. Man resembles the monkeys. Although this is true. man also resembles aliens from space who seem to periodically crash into the Earth from other galaxies. You might consider that this is indeed funny. Actually, you need nitrogen or nitrous oxide to laugh. The aliens arriving here from space did not intend to stay here for some reason or other, possibly because of so much nitrogen or other substances in our atmosphere. They may have decided to advance the genetics of Earth's monkeys into a living creature more similar to themselves. At any rate, none of us were alive back then to be star witnesses.

David, a young Hebrew, managed to kill the giant Goliath with a small rock. How very smart that was. Suddenly, weapons meant more than muscle, and the very smart killed the less smart.

This new phenomenon called war spread to Europe as men with weapons killed animals for fur coats to stay warm in a glacier environment with cold rain. The glaciers kept receding, and some Europeans out on peninsulas were stranded there as the seas rose from the melting ice and global warming.

What good fortune to be a civilized Englishman or Irishman and be cut off from the rest of warmongering Europe! Still, there were waves of Scandinavians in boats looking to plunder near and far. They even made it to North America, but Asians had already crossed the Bering land bridge and beaten them there to become North American Indian tribes.

The English were raped by these Vikings and bore more Viking descendents. Soon all of Europe was building boats and setting sail, bringing war to the rest of the world. The Chinese had built much larger boats and discovered Africa two hundred years earlier, but one emperor there decided to scrap the entire fleet because he didn't want the Africans to discover China.

Therefore it was those Europeans who colonized most of the world. From the Philippines to the South Pole to North and South America, there came these Europeans who spoke European languages, and thus we had two world wars as various European factions had perfected mass production of weapons systems. European man was like Cain, who killed Abel in the Bible, completely remorseless.

These wars were all fought without end, and many speculated that the world would soon end with one big bang from atomic weapons or the like. Man was mass-producing everything in a great industrial and postindustrial revolution fueled by supply and demand. Demand was created by consumerism and overpopulation, which began to tax the planet with too much carbon dioxide, creating global warming, tornados, hurricanes, and even earthquakes from fracking to produce oil.

It looked as if the Earth might very soon be destroyed if everything continued in momentum. Then some new viruses appeared to level the playing field.

Viruses had been around a very long time, maybe forever. When the population of France was five million, England four million, and Russia three million, that was only six hundred years ago. Nowadays, the world population is forty times greater at least. Where there were ten people in every square mile, now there are four hundred. This is where the viruses can raise some havoc with a species that intermingles and goes downtown shopping.

Now we have entered the long overdue Great Reduction we knew was coming. Here, we have it in the SARS-CoV-2 virus. I would complain that we deserve such a fate. It was inevitable that Mother Earth would want to clean up all this carbon dioxide and foul air we have created.

Surely this is not our fault; we were just born. True, but our ancestors, those Europeans who have been exploiting the planet's resources ...

We are the inheritors of this big, toxic mess, including plastics swirling in all the oceans and so much global warming from carbon dioxide, creating class-5 hurricanes. This is all our very rich history for better or worse, finally turned for the worse.

ALL THAT DRAINS DOWN THE SINKHOLE MIGHT BE OUR FORMER FREEDOM AS WELL

ACREDIBLE PRESIDENT WOULD BE ABLE TO LEAD THE COUNTRY OUT OF this pandemic and lockdown.

However, because he is incredible and that means no one believes him, he is barely able to find his way out of a paper bag. So stay there, Mr. President.

The governors of each state were asked to decide whether they might put each respective state in lockdown. Now the governors feel it should be their individual decisions when to unlock each state.

Our incredible president is announcing it will be his own tremendous decision when states decide anything at all. His incompetence has been blamed for this human catastrophe reaching our shores, so we Americans are hesitant to trust his authority, his word, or his deeds.

He is a too self-righteous ignoramus, to put it mildly. The American people think they deserve better than this. How did our system fail to bring this spoiled brat to power in the first place?

The American people are led by their television networks and advertising. Therefore, any spoiled brat with his own jet plane and limousine impresses their materialistic attitude. A great consumer must be a great person in the American way of thinking. Wrong again.

So let us concentrate and plan our way out of this debacle partly caused by the pharmocracy and doctocracy we have let take over our government of mostly corporations and their investors first and everybody else last.

> Dear God,
> Just what is this giant mess we have encouraged to take shape and mess up our lives big time?

> Sincerely,
> We the people

> P.S., Contact tracing of all positive COVID-19 patients will be a brand-new giant industry, like the secret police or the KGB.

THE PEST AND THE
PESTILENCE

If a US president is a criminal

Whose political party will not remove him from office as say by impeachment,

Can his political party be held accountable

For his crimes against the American people,

His obstruction of justice, and his crimes against the environment?

So may the US citizens themselves enter a lawsuit

For the people, by the people, and of the people

For all damages incurred by his presidency, which they illegitimize

For his crimes against the people, the nation, and all humanity,

Which is bound together in mutual peace by certain laws.

These truths and rights are self-evident and sustainable in a court of law

By our Father, who is in heaven, and on the Earth as well, to regulate by commandments.

So help us God if we can no longer help ourselves,

As if the devil has overwhelmed us with some pestilence.

May indeed the pests upon our society be removed and quarantined.

May we be restored to health, which is our natural right to pursue happiness.

May God intervene on our behalf to correct this grievous calamity and pestilence,

For the sake of righteousness that peace be restored and wars cease.

So help us God, if there is no justice, this shall be the end of our civilized world,

Because the barbarians have come to sack Jerusalem to make it a desolation for wild hyenas only.

Therefore weep and wear sackcloth because your riches cannot save you or me.

The destruction will be complete; there will be an entire annihilation

Of this perverse race, of these perverse people, and their perverse political parties and systems

That corrupt justice and make this land abhorrent and an abomination.

Cleanse us, O Lord our God. Restore to us your divine purity,

That we see truly again your self-evident truth,

So our consciousness can be clear and free, and may corruption leave us, and God save us

From ourselves and such a political party of hoodlums and thugs.

Send them up the river where they belong, with their devil, into a prison,

For at least one thousand years if not more.

Because it is written that you shall see God.

His truth is everlasting, and his victory shall come with the sword of his mouth, His truth.

Printed in the United States
By Bookmasters